JOHN LUCY ASH

The Nexus Prince

The Dragonbinder Chronicles: Book One

First edition

ISBN: 9798218933531

Cover art by Ace Sadler, ESP
Illustration by Ace Sadler, ESP

This book was professionally typeset on Reedsy.
Find out more at reedsy.com

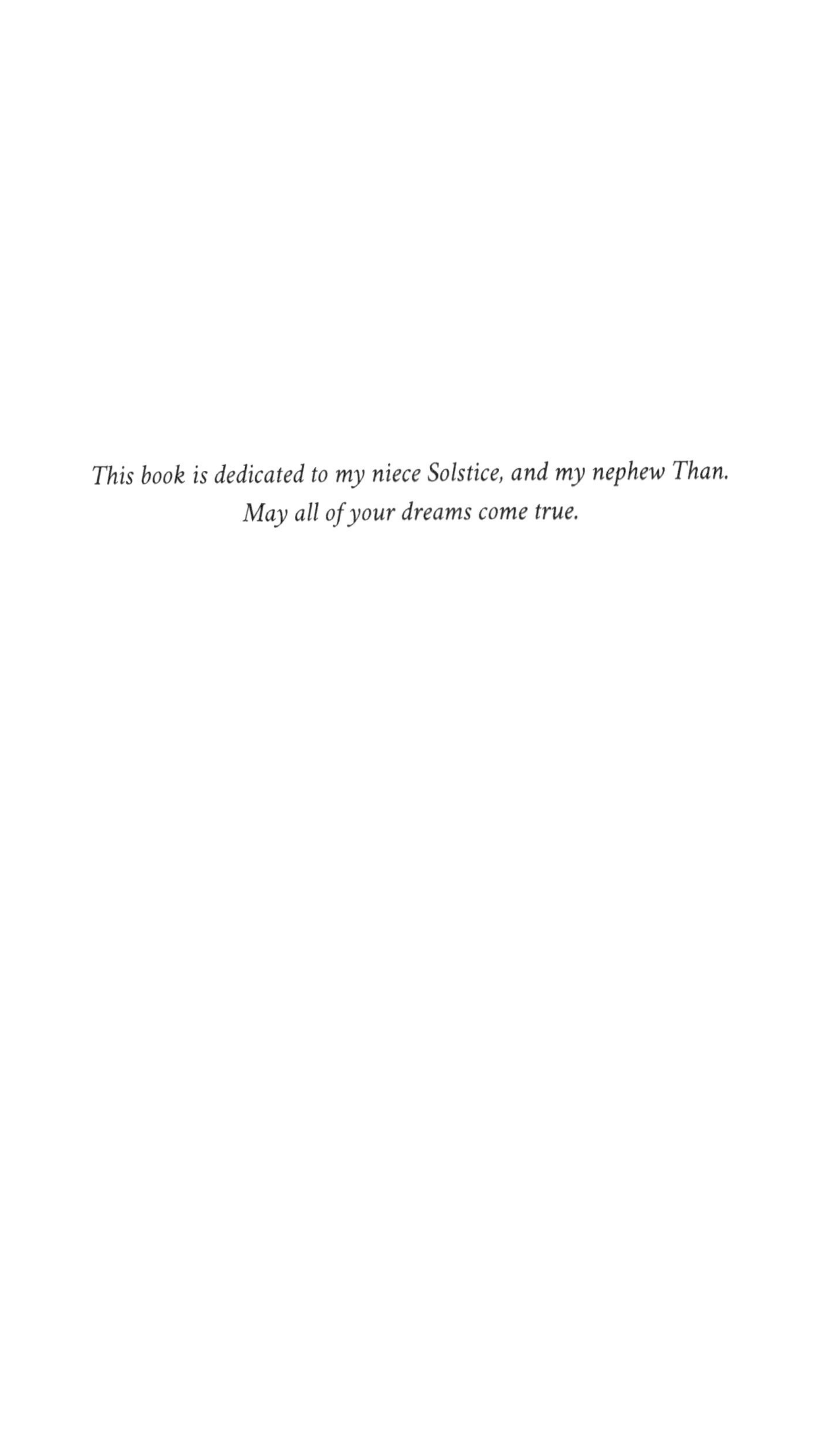

This book is dedicated to my niece Solstice, and my nephew Than.
May all of your dreams come true.

"I count myself in nothing else so happy as in
a soul remembering my good friends."

William Shakespeare, Richard II, 2.3.46

Contents

Foreword

"I honestly love it. I think that The Nexus Prince feels like Douglas Adams, George R.R. Martin and J.R.R. Tolkien got together and decided to write the next young adult blockbuster, but I don't feel like that is giving enough credit for creativity. Because Ash truly does have a voice that is all his own, and unlike any other authors." -Christi W.

"In my 66th year circling around our sun, traveling across the city can be challenging but *The Nexus Prince* made transcending dimensions effortlessly flawless, exhilarating and very entertaining. Couldn't put it down." -Donna P.

"It is not often that I read something that I can't put down. I was closely involved in the psychological aspects of this book, and I really enjoyed…Your book had me reading to the last page." -Yvonne H.

"I really enjoyed reading this, man." -Ace S.

"It's perfect." -Lia W.

"A wonderfully complex fantasy that combines comedy, psychological depth, and dual-reality world building in a unique, character-driven debut." -Anonymous.

Preface

I wrote this novel as a way of coping with my own personal grief, after losing several friends throughout my life. I wanted to try to find a way to explain the feelings associated with that loss, and share them in a way that might help others. My purpose in writing this book was cathartic. It helped to heal me, and I'm hoping it may help you a little as well, if you need a little healing for your own journey.

It was always a dream of mine to be a writer, and after a near death experience, I decided to make my dream a reality. I had fallen down a 20 foot flight of stairs, suffered from 7 broken bones and had internal bleeding in my brain.

Recovery from that was not easy, it took one step at a time. I had to learn how to walk again, talk again, and how to believe in myself again. By the grace of God, I was able to heal through that journey, and become stronger than I was before in every way. I share this with you, because I truly believe all things are possible. If I can go from a severe brain injury to writing a novel, maybe you will someday find it within yourself to follow your dreams too.

So, what is *The Nexus Prince* about anyways? One of the biggest lessons that my late friend Susan taught me, is that family isn't necessarily who we are born with, but the people we meet along the way. You will know your family by how they make you feel. And family is everything. Ultimately, that is what this story is about. A young man that doesn't feel like he has a family finds one in the form of a motley crew of strangers.

Acknowledgments

Thank you to all the ones who were lost too soon. For Kyle, Susan, Seth, Allie, Marlena, Melanie, and Beeker. You were more than just friends, you were family.

Thank you to all of my teachers, from Kindergarten to earning my M.S.

Mr. Keene, for teaching me how to write creatively, and how to believe in myself.

Mr. Beavers, thank you for teaching me that it's not about the piece of paper, it's what you do with it that counts.

Ms. DePrimo, for encouraging me to continue when I was at an all-time low, and endowing me with the skills to succeed.

Ms. Evert, for putting me in the math club.

Ms. Harris, for teaching me how to read.

Jane, for teaching me how to be courageous.

And Wanda, for letting me take your daughter to prom.

And to all the librarians, for being the keepers of knowledge, and for helping the world to be a better place, one book at a time.

Introduction

From a fragment of a torn and burnt page of Codex IV in The Grand Crystal Archives:

<u>The World of Here Beyond</u>
When twin moons eat the sun's last light,
And dragons fade from fearful sight,
Then from the world of wire and stone,
A lonely, two-souled king shall roam.
Not crowned in gold, nor armed with steel,
But bearing wounds that are too real.
The star-drake's purr, the moss-man's sigh,
The courage of a fading cry.
The friend, the sprite, the memory's power,
Will all align that fateful hour.
Singing crystals to the Nexus Prince hark,
Awake the light that sleeps in dark.
He binds not dragon, but the bond—
The final truth, so deep, so fond,
sings to the world of here beyond.

I

Part One

Here There Be Dragons

1

Smells Like Drake Magic

Pet dragons come with all sorts of problems.

The biggest problem with having a miniature purple plushie star-dotted dragon sleeping on your structural engineering textbook was not the otherworldly smell of magic, or the way its obsidian claws occasionally twitched and scored the glossy cover: The problem was the drool. And dragon drool is nothing like the saliva of humans, or even dogs for that matter. While most creatures drool would be just a minor nuisance, drake spit is copious amounts of gooey, oozing slime, with a somewhat-off odor reliably present.

A tiny, shimmering, glittery puddle of what looked like liquid starlight was slowly spreading from the dragon's maw, seeping into the pages detailing load-bearing tensile strengths. Harvey Chandler watched it from his desk chair, a half-eaten slice of cold pepperoni pizza forgotten in his hand. He called the dragon Spitfire, a name he felt was both accurate and, in a private, bitter way, hilarious due to the dragon lacking the ability to spit fire. The only thing it spit was, well—spit.

"You're going to short-circuit the entire concept of post-and-lintel construction," he murmured, his voice a dry rasp from too much coffee and not enough human conversation. Harvey was only upset briefly, until he remembered the fact that he was going to skip over that section entirely anyways.

Spitfire, whose actual form was that of a perfectly normal, if slightly dusty, fluffy toy to anyone else, let out a soft *chuff-chuff* sound in its sleep. He was sure he was the only college freshman with such an otherworldly plush in their possession.

Harvey was an average young man, bespectacled and unassuming. He wasn't handsome, or cute. He wasn't ugly either, just average in just about every way. He was thin and wiry, one of his foster mothers would tell him he needed to eat more. "Skin and bones!" She would don him at nearly every holiday meal. Most of his classmates didn't know he even existed, that is how average his existence was. Just another seat to be filled, in any given auditorium.

Harvey was just about average in every way, except for the fact that at his age he still had a purple plushy dragon doll.

Although Harvey was average, his name was not. Not average at all, not by any stretch of the imagination. In his entire life, he had never met another Harvey. He had not even heard of any Harveys who had lived before. There were Harrys, Jims, Jacks and Johns and even Jons, but no Harveys. He was the only Harvey.

Even with its rarity, many of his teachers would need to be reminded of his name, even after teaching him for months or years, that's how mundane and bizarre the name Harvey was. Sometimes they would just point to him and say "young man" or "you." His Quantum Art Theory Professor had even called him Carlos Montoya Esteban the III, once. Which is slightly different from the name Harvey, but Harvey still responded to it. Even the frames of his glasses would even sometimes forget that they were attached to his face, and they would just slide right off the bridge of his nose, as if they had been held up by nobody at all.

The bioluminescent moss that Harvey saw crawling up the far corner wall in his living room pulsed with a sympathetic, gentle blue light. He'd named the different moss patches. The one by the window was Steve. Steve was a pessimistic shade of blue today.

Oh, Steve.

Perhaps moss wasn't supposed to grow inside of apartments in general, but perhaps that wasn't the case with college students. In fact, you would be astounded by the things that consistently appear in most campus dorms. New species of viruses, insects, and sometimes startup tech companies are some of the things that might show up randomly.

So, upon additional review, it has been found that the predetermined notion that Harvey was average is not an accurate depiction, no not at all. Harvey was not average, he was about as odd as they come.

With a sigh that was more performance art than genuine annoyance, Harvey set the slice down, wiped his fingers on his jeans, and carefully slid the textbook out from under the sleeping celestial reptile. The drool stretched in pearlescent strings before snapping. This was pet dragon ownership in a nutshell, cleaning up massive amounts of slimy drool. "How many trees shall we tear down to clean up your mess today, Spitfire?"

He snagged a roll of paper towels—the boring, beige cheaper kind that Harvey's roommate stole from under the dorm cafeteria sink—from under his desk and dabbed at the book, then at the dragon's chin. Spitfire nuzzled into the touch, its scales warm and impossibly smooth and bumpy under his fingers. Real. It always felt so real. Sometimes he forgot that he was the only one that could see Spitfire that way.

Across the room, in the reality everyone else shared (or so Harvey assumed), his chubby, comic-obsessed roommate Leo was attempting to assemble a piece of IKEA furniture. The sound of a mallet hitting particle board was a percussive counterpoint to the soft, chiming hum of the apartment's fantasy layer. Drum. Drum. Drum. The doldrums of the conundrum of the drumming continued mercilessly.

"I swear to Zeus," Leo grunted, his voice muffled by what sounded like a mouthful of screws. "The Swedes are punishing us for our colonial past. This is a cultural reckoning in the form of a Björkön bookshelf." Leo's tummy erupted from under his too-tight faded superhero t-shirt. Harvey was not even sure who this particular superhero was. Deodorant Man? The Tulip? It didn't matter. He was certain it would be a superhero t-shirt, even if he couldn't make out who it was from this distance. Leo only dressed one way. Sweatpants. Superhero t-shirt. Slide-on slip-resistant wide-foot shoe wear. It was predictable, and the formula was never abandoned, not even for special occasions.

"The instructions are just pictures, Leo," Harvey said, not looking up from his drool-stained book.

"These aren't pictures, man. They're hieroglyphs. A universal language of confusion. A warning from a dying civilization." Leo emerged from behind a leaning tower of shelves, his dark hair dusted with a fine wood-shaving snowfall. Harvey did wonder how a hammer could produce so many wood shavings. He was using a hammer, wasn't he?

The truth was, it could have been a saw, or a drill, or a matter displacement pad. Harvey was not good with tools, or even vaguely aware of how to use them. This was disheartening at times, but he was thankful that he lived in modern times, and did not have to compete with Neanderthalensis. Proving his speedy prowess with tools as an evolutionary advantage might be a challenge. Harvey couldn't blame his lack of knowledge here on poor vision, or the lack of a father figure to show him how. He just had never been one for fixing things. He didn't care. Breaking them, on the other hand...

Leo was a film major, which meant he approached all of life's problems as if they were a poorly directed third act. He squinted at Harvey. "Are you playing with your little dragon buddy again? You really should see someone about that. Super weird bro."

Harvey's spine went rigid. He casually dropped his hand from Spitfire's head. "Oh, I'm just taking a break from this textbook. I have a big assignment due in the morning and I just can't focus at all." Spitfire playfully stuck his tongue out at Harvey.

"Gotcha." Leo hefted a wooden dowel like a tiny club. "Well, tell your subconscious to manifest a socket wrench. I think I'm missing one."

"I would help look for one for you if I had any idea what a socket wrench looked like.

"It's a miracle you've made it this far." Leo chuckled.

"I hear that a lot, actually." Harvey chimed, truthfully.

As Leo retreated back into his battle with Scandinavian design, Harvey's gaze drifted to the window. Outside, the city of Madison was doing its thing under a gray, drizzling sky. It was a typical Midwestern hub of lakes and tech-dreams. Cars honked, a siren wailed in the distance. But superimposed over it, Harvey saw the Glimmering Spires of the Silvan Deeps, their crystalline peaks catching a light from a sun that wasn't there. A sky-whale, looking like a bloated, benevolent zeppelin, drifted serenely past the Prudential Center. He'd learned to ignore the cognitive dissonance. It was like seeing a persistent, beautiful, and utterly terrifying Magic Eye picture etched permanently onto the world.

His phone buzzed. A notification from his calendar glowed across the cold screen, its image stark and digital against the dual-layered reality:

```
Don't forget - Therapist appt — Dr. Evans — 4:00 PM.
```

The appointment loomed in his mind, a black hole around which the rest of his day would inevitably collapse. He looked at Spitfire, now awake and blinking its star-filled eyes at him. It butted its head against his hand, a silent request for more attention. Harvey felt a familiar, crushing wave of affection and despair.

This was his mind. This beautiful, broken, impossible creation. Dr. Evans and the little orange pills in his bathroom cabinet called it a "dissociative coping mechanism." A "rich inner fantasy life triggered by trauma and sustained by a neurodivergent psyche." They used words like "psychosis" and "treatment" and "management."

To Harvey, it felt more like he was a radio receiver poorly tuned to two stations at once, and the medication just filled the space between them with a distant static dissonance. It didn't make the fantasy station go away; it just made all the signals painful to listen to. The annoying whisper grew into a roaring like the hiss on the in-between channels on a television set in the 1980s.

He got up, the chair groaning in relief. Spitfire, the Star-Dragon hopped off the desk, its wings—translucent membranes holding entire constellations—fluttering silently. It padded after him as he walked to the kitchen, its passage causing the whimsical dust bunnies under the sofa to swirl in a way that, to Harvey, looked like miniature galaxies being born and dying.

In the kitchen, the dissonance channel between worlds was particularly strong. The humming fridge was covered in Leo's takeout menus and punk rock basement show posters. Harvey saw them, but he also saw the runic carvings of the Larder-Mage, glowing with faint preservation spells. He opened the fridge. A half-empty carton of milk, a six-pack of beer, a wilting head of lettuce. And on the top shelf, sitting right next to Leo's expensive Greek yogurt, was a cluster of dreamberries, plump and glowing with a soft violet light. They were Spitfire's favorite, and they tasted like a fiber-rich bubble gum.

He plucked out a handful of the berries for Spitfire. To anyone else (or to Leo, for that matter), he was just standing there, holding an empty hand, looking like a crazy person. He placed a few of the large, plump dreamberries on the floor. Spitfire chirped, sounding of wind chimes made of crystal, and began to nibble at the immaculate fruit.

Nomf nompf neruuumph.

Leo walked in, holding the Björkön instruction sheet as if it were a sacred scroll. "Dude. We're out of milk again. And I'm pretty sure this thing is going to be a permanent leaning tower of Pisa." He glanced down at the floor where Spitfire was eating. "Did you drop something?"

Harvey shoved his hands in his pockets. "Just… checking the linoleum for structural integrity."

Leo gave him a long, unreadable look. It wasn't a suspicion, exactly. It was more a kind of weary, fond bafflement. "You are the weirdest roommate I have ever had, and I once lived with a guy who collected his own nail clippings in a mason jar. You know that, right?"

"It's my cross to bear," Harvey said, the ghost of a smile touching his lips. Harvey stood up and saw a group of young people walking by outside the front window. Another group of young people was walking past them going the opposite direction. None of them saw each other, they all just stared down at their cellular phones, transfixed to the digital world they had convinced themselves was worth their time and energy. "I don't know if being weird in this world is necessarily a bad thing, Leo. I truly wonder sometimes."

He thought about the young people not interacting, not saying hello. Not giving life a chance. What if they were supposed to be friends, or even lovers? What if two of the people in that group were soulmates, but they would never even know because they were too busy checking their notifications to see how many "likes" they had this hour, so they never even took the time to say hello?

Harvey's smile didn't last, as he pondered such things. His eyes drifted past Leo, through the kitchen doorway, to the small table by the front door where his keys, wallet, and the plastic orange prescription bottle full of orange tablets that tasted like plastic sat waiting. He wondered if the pills tasted like plastic because they spent so much time being housed inside of a plastic bottle. Or what if he was swallowing pieces of the pill bottle rather than the pills themselves, and he was just hallucinating the difference? These seemed like completely normal every day questions to Harvey.

The little bottle seemed to pulse with a malevolent energy all its own, a dark star in the constellation of his daily life. But unlike Spitfire, the pill bottle was not decorated with stars. Only labels and warnings. They didn't seem as fun as the ones in the commercials. The bottle just said "Be careful driving or operating heavy machinery."

The commercials would say things like: "If your eyes start bleeding uncontrollably and you suddenly believe you are a dead hamster, please let your physician know. Common side effects include constipation, headaches, stomach cramps and unexpected impregnation by wild pollen." In a few hours, he would have to sit in Dr. Evans' overly warm office and lie about how much better he'd been feeling.

19 Years Ago:

"Either you or your child are not going to make it. I'm sorry, it's one or the other." The nurse enlightened Elizabeth Chandler of the tragic situation. Her heart swelled with sorrow, yet she already knew the choice she would make. Of course, there was only one possible choice in this situation.

Philip Chandler reached in his pocket and felt a pack of cigarettes. He couldn't pull one out at this moment, but he found comfort in reminding himself that they were there. His decision would have been different than Elizabeth's, as she meant the world to him.

"I choose him." Elizabeth proclaimed.

A great hurt overcame Philip as he sobbed. He knew she was making the right choice, but he couldn't bear the thought of losing her. She meant the world to him. He couldn't imagine life without her beauty in it.

Elizabeth pointed to the book on the shelf she had been writing. "It's for him, you must see that he reads it." She pleaded.

The nurse nodded, and Philip looked over to the manuscript. He knew she had been writing for some time, but he had never read it. He wasn't much of a reader, anyways. Reading was for intellects, and although he did have a proper education, he did not consider himself among their company.

He was an every day American man, he spent his time working with his hands and getting dirty. Trying to provide for his love and for his future child. Now he wondered if any of it had been worth his time. Why did he work so hard to build a future for his family that he now was hearing would simply not exist?

Hours later, after Elizabeth had passed away, he found himself staring into their baby's eyes. He had her eyes. Philip walked away, and he never saw his child again. He was haunted by the memory of his beloved wife, and could not bear to even think of her anymore. Seeing their child would simply add salt to the wound of such profound loss.

He walked, and he walked. He walked for so long, he found himself in a desert. His shoes had given way to the elements, and the skin of his toes was now becoming calloused from the blistering, red sand. He wept until his tears were as dry as the desert.

His eyes hurt, but he found solace in feeling something, anything other than loss. He had found, gained this suffering. He earned it, and he smiled as he fell to the ground. A scorpion walked across the desert floor, perilously close to his face, yet Philip was too weak to move.

That is all that was known about the disappearance of Philip Chandler.

2

Several Thousand Feet Above a Sea of Boiling Mist

In the city of Madison, the capital building was the center of it all. It was the place where people would take their children, where they would gaze up at the renaissance-inspired art work from yesteryear, painted and placed at impossibly high heights upon glossy marbled walls. The building was stoic and grandeur, yet the illusion of superiority would fade if you walked into the public bathrooms, which smelled like aged bureaucratic urine, worse than any typical bathroom.

Although the building was haughty, the city's people were humble and kind. They cared for one another, and enjoyed simpler things in life, like drinking, social get-togethers, and biking. There was always an event or two going on, art fairs, farmer's markets, live-music festivals. None of those things appealed to Harvey, he spent most of his time just holed up in his room, reading a book or playing a video game.

Beyond the wall of dissonant plasma, in the land called the Aetherium, there existed a parallel city called Nosidam. In a parallel location of the capital building, the Charred Council's Citadel floated several thousand feet above a sea of boiling mist, its architecture seeming to defy gravity, sanity, and several other of Isaac Newton's more popular suggestions.

The gargoyles that covered the citadel from top to bottom weren't decorative. They were functional, in the way a landmine is functional. They perched on spires of black basalt, their stone hides steaming in the perpetual twilight rain, and their job was to detect inter dimensional interlopers.

Harvey Chandler, drenched and shivering in a once-white, now stained with the dust of eons of in-between-time t-shirt and torn, tattered jeans, was the very definition of an interloper. He'd been trying to find a dry spot under a leering, dolphin-headed grotesque gargoyle for the past ten minutes, but the rain, which tasted different on his tongue in this new place, had a nasty habit of changing direction.

The rain was warm, but he was covered in so much of it, it made him feel cold the moment there would be a lapse of downpour. The blanket of the warm droplets was quickly missed.

You could never actually dress prepared for the weather in Madison, because it was completely unpredictable. One time it snowed in May on a warm summer day. All the beautiful blooming flowers died from the bitter frost. And it was not unusual for it to suddenly be sunny and warm in the middle of winter.

But the people of Madison had a different idea of comfort, weather-wise. The college students would prance around shirtless, tossing a football outside and having a beer with their friends gleefully when the weather would rise from 18 degrees to a mere 37 degree "heat wave."

"This is a new low, even for you," he muttered to himself, wiping water from his eyes. "How punk do you have to be to find comfort in the rain? Isn't there a song about that?" There was a song about that, actually. And it was written by a band from Madison, ironically. Or perhaps there was nothing ironic about it at all.

His head throbbed, a deep, resonant ache centered behind his left temple. It was the same headache he'd had since the car accident, a constant, dull reminder that his reality was now officially a two-lane highway with a collapsed bridge in the middle.

Back on the other lane, the one with traffic laws and physics that mostly made sense, his 2008 Honda Civic was probably being towed to a scrapyard where it would be melted down and reborn as something useful, like a toaster.

Toast. Mmm. Extra burnt with butter, peanut butter and grape jelly. Some people thought the extra step of butter before peanut butter was just too much, but not Harvey. He knew that was the secret ingredient to culinary bliss. That could be true for just about any kind of dish, pastry or even drink.

Just add Better Butter, butter to make it better. Are you convinced yet? Insert paid advertisement space right here, the future of fiction. Okay sorry folks, just had to break the fourth wall to bring you this word from our sponsors. It's the future of future advertising, haven't you heard?

Shout out to **Better Butter** *butter: Your favorite bodacious creamery, building butts that barely fit in extra large brown-colored pants since 1953!*

June 20, 2002

The final review for his term paper for Arch 451: Advanced Structural Systems had been going well. Professor Turing, a man whose face was a topographical map of academic disappointment, had actually nodded twice at his presentation on cantilevered support for urban hydroponic farms. Even one nod would have been a notable achievement from Professor Turing.

Harvey sped home, noticing his classmate Brenda walking on the side of the road. He always had a bit of a crush on Brenda, but he was too shy and nervous to actually do anything about it. She was beautiful to him, starry blue eyes, soft pale skin, and her most attractive quality was her kind demeanor. She was always exceptionally sweet and gentle to Harvey, far more than he felt he deserved. His dream was to ask her out on a date someday, but he also didn't really want to go on a date at all.

Harvey's ideal evening would be laying around, watching a movie or playing a game with Spitfire on his lap. This was not something that most of his peers found entertaining, by any stretch of the imagination. They were usually out partying, going to sporting events, eating the deep fried wings whilst yelling at the screen that the guys in green should definitely have beat the guys in blue.

He tried socializing that way a few times, and found it to be incredibly awkward. He felt like a sociologist out in the field, researching a strange group of never before seen beings. Their testosterone would surge, the blood would rage in their veins, they would stand, cheer, hug each other, punch each other, threaten each other. And these things were all done as a kind of camaraderie. It was all so bizarre to Harvey.

Suddenly his thoughts were interrupted, as a six-armed red and black glowing shadow-demon had slithered down from the Glimmering Spires and phase-shifted through his windshield, shrieking. Harvey had swerved. A fire hydrant had not. The last thing he remembered from that day was the taste of blood and the sound of his classmate named Brenda screaming, "I think he's seizing!"

But he wasn't seizing. He was being evicted from one reality and dumped into another. That was the moment Harvey's ability to perceive two worlds began. It was a painful birth that looked unpleasant, and was in actuality— unpleasant.

As stated before, this was the moment that it started. But Harvey didn't think that could be entirely sure of that. He had moments all throughout his life where odd things happened, where bits of magic floated through the world before him. Sometimes it was a moment, a color, a song. It usually happened upon deep reflection, like when he thought about not knowing his parents, and how he longed for that connection.

A door, heavy and made of a wood that seemed to be slowly petrifying into bone appeared out of nowhere, creaking open further down the rampart. A figure emerged, silhouetted against the flickering torchlight from within. It was a woman, tall and clad in aged leather armor that looked both practical and uncomfortably tight. Her hair was the color of a storm cloud and shaved on one side. The other side fell over an eye that was currently glaring at him with the warmth of a tax audit. She looked like an emo extra from any given local renaissance fair.

"Are you coming or not?" she asked. Her voice was flat, devoid of any curiosity. She had a strength in her voice, and her dirt-coated, fiery auburn hair showed she was not afraid to work hard. She held a crossbow, but not in a threatening way. It was more like she was just holding it, the way a person might hold a set of keys, and the fact that it was a weapon capable of punching a hole through a refrigerator was merely a secondary characteristic.

"Who are you?" Harvey offered, giving her a weak smile. "And where are we exactly? I'm very confused."

"My name is Kael. The question is, who are you? You don't belong here! The Aetherium has no tolerance for outsiders."

"Kael? Like the lettuce?"

"Mock my name again and I will skin you." Kael said, and Harvey believed her. "Hmm. So we are in agreement on me not belonging here. I just don't know where 'here' is, or how I got here in the first place." Harvey looked around at the different colors than what he was used to. He glanced at his own hand and saw it looked to be the same as before. (That was a relief).

"The Mists of Lament do not 'let up.' If you don't walk towards me now and come through the gate fully, the stream between two worlds will tear you apart in a matter of moments!"

"Believe me, I'm working on getting out of here. I don't think I'm supposed to go with you, I've been trying to... think myself back. It's not really working though." He'd discovered that intense concentration, combined with a desperate desire to be anywhere else, was occasionally resulting in what he could only describe as a flicker. A momentary glimpse-perhaps a flashback-of a sterile white ceiling and the beep of a heart monitor. Then the headache would spike, and he'd be back in the rain.

The beautiful woman adorned in ragged aged leather sighed. It was a long-suffering sound. "The trans-dimensional flux is stabilizing. Your presence is a splinter in the flesh of this world. The more you try to force it out, the more the world tries to push you out. And if that doesn't work, I will push you out myself violently."

"I have no idea what that means, but thanks? So, what, are you saying I'm a metaphysical splinter? That's a new one. My therapist usually goes with 'adaptive sycophantic daydreaming.' And what are you supposed to be, exactly? Some sort of guardian for this place?"

"I am a member of the Octavian Guard. More specifically, I am a time warden and I represent The Charred Council. And yes we guard and protect the realm of Aetherium." Kael's good eye, a sharp, flinty gray, scanned the misty chasm below. "You are an anomaly here. An uninvited guest. The Council has enough problems without a reality-challenged mortal dripping all over the place. We need to figure out how to get you home now."

As if to punctuate her point, a deep, guttural roar echoed from somewhere in the mist-shrouded distance. It wasn't a sound of animal fury; it was a sound of profound, ancient agony. The very stones of the citadel trembled. The rain sizzled where it hit the walls. Harvey's headache flared, a white-hot needle driven directly into his brain stem. He gasped, stumbling against the wet parapet.

Harvey gasped at the sound, it was so loud he felt it vibrate every atom in his body. Kael didn't flinch. She just watched him, her expression unchanging. "That sound is one of the most powerful dragons, Eranthus, who is slowly passing from this realm. A technocratic technomancer named Turing harpoons him daily, siphoning his essence to power their wretched cities. His pain is constant. You will learn to ignore it, or you will go mad." She paused. "If you are not already mad."

"You mean Professor Turing? He's just a typical college professor. How could he have anything to do with that sound?" Harvey grunted, straightening up. The pain was receding, leaving a phantom echo of that roar in his skull.

His mind tried to come to terms with the sound he had just heard. A dragon? They had a dying dragon here. Of course they did. I guess it made sense, in that nothing at all made any sense here. This place was like a Tolkien novel written by someone on a bad acid trip.

Suddenly, the air above him crackled. It wasn't lightning. It was a different kind of energy, sharp and artificial. A spear of pure, blinding red and white light lanced up from the mist below. It moved with impossible speed and precision, striking something massive and unseen in the storm-wracked sky. There was a silent, concussive flash.

And then, the voice.

It wasn't a sound that traveled through the air. It was a thought, a memory, a command, branded directly onto the surface of his consciousness. It was the sound of a mountain breaking, of a star going cold. It was a death-scream, and it had words. It was the voice of a dragon.

DRAGONBINDER.

Harvey screamed. It was a raw, tearing sound that was swallowed by the rain and the stone. He fell to his knees, clutching his head. This was no hallucination. This was an invasion. It was a cognitive root canal without anesthetic. The word—dragonbinder—the accusation that Eranthus charged at him with that word echoed in the vault of his mind, scouring everything in its path. What on Earth is a dragonbinder? Harvey looked up at the dark violet midday sky. Well, perhaps Harvey could rephrase his question, since he clearly was not on Earth.

When the world swam back into focus, he was on all fours, vomiting what little was in his stomach onto the ancient, rain-slicked stones. It was just water. He hadn't eaten in this world. He didn't even know if he could.

He looked up, his vision blurry. Kael was still there, yet she offered him no comfort. Her crossbow was now pointed at his chest. Her face, for the first time, showed an emotion other than weary contempt. It was a cold, sharp shock. A flicker of something that looked almost like fear. "What did it tell you?" She demanded to know.

"It said dragonbinder. What does that mean?" Harvey asked her.

Back in the other realm, in the sterile white room, a nurse was adjusting the IV in Harvey's arm. His body lay still on the infirmary bed, the steady beep-beep-beep rattle-tattle of the heart monitor a testament to a life in stable, mundane suspension. A doctor shined a penlight into his unseeing eyes, noting the fixed, dilated pupils. "Post-traumatic fugue state," he dictated to a junior intern. "Likely non-epileptic seizure disorder, psychosomatic in origin. We'll need a full neurological work-up."

He had no way of knowing that his patient, at that exact moment, was on his knees in another dimension, with a crossbow aimed at his heart, the psychic death-scream of a dragon god still ringing in his ears, and a single, impossible word now permanently etched into the core of his being.

Dragonbinder...

Kael lowered her crossbow, and looked at the boy, puzzled. "That's not possible...Are you really one of them? You don't look like a dragonbinder. You just look like a loser, sorry no offense." The expression on her face suddenly changed as she seemed to decide that it might be a possibility. "Your kind are not welcome here, go back to where you came from!" She raised her hands and they were glowing with a frightening violet. She shoved Harvey and he suddenly found himself plopped down back on Earth. He knew he was home the moment he saw a piece of litter floating across the ground. It was a newspaper, and the wind blew its pages to and fro frantically.

The text that sprawled across the paper read *"Turing discovers new energy source using quantum computing."*

Days passed. They turned into weeks. Months. Years. It all seemed the same, and everything felt irrelevant. Harvey thought of nothing other than the other world he had stumbled onto. He dreamed of the day when he could go back and solve the mysteries of what he had experienced. He simultaneously wanted nothing to do with it at all. A part of him, a large part of him, wished none of it had happened. It left him with more questions than answers, and he just felt unsure of everything.

His healing from the accident had taken some time. Days to talk again. Months to walk again. He thought he must be back to his old self eventually, but he was also entirely unsure. He didn't remember if there was a difference, and he didn't know anyone that cared enough to let him know otherwise.

The real world just felt boring now. It had less color, and everything felt dull. Even his favorite foods lost their appeal. A part of him just dreaded everything. So he stayed away from everyone else. He found himself falling behind in his studies, as he just didn't care anymore.

3

Bathing in a Shimmering, Non-corporeal Sunbeam

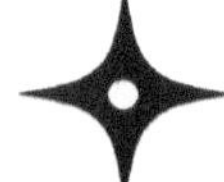

The new pills were the color of a faded bruise and tasted like chalky, forgotten promises. Harvey dry-swallowed two of them, leaning against the cool, fake-marble of his bathroom counter. He avoided the mirror. Mirrors had become… complicated. Sometimes his reflection winked. Sometimes it had scales.

"You should take your medications with a glass of water" his mother had always told him. But his mother wasn't here anymore. Harvey's mother had passed away a few years ago, and he had never met his father.

He had heard his father lived in California as a drugged-out vagrant. That was something he did not aspire to mimic, but he worried that someday he might. Did the addict gene skip a generation? Who knows.

He missed them often, especially around holidays. Well, he missed his mother. He missed the idea of his father, at least he had for most of his childhood. He had given up on any fantasy of meeting him someday, it just wasn't worth the time and energy.

Harvey wondered if he had experienced mild delusions on and off his whole life (what artist hasn't), or if they only appeared after the car crash that led to his severe head injury. The more he pondered it, the more he was certain that what he had just experienced was just a delusion. There was no Kael, no giant dragon speaking to him in a booming voice. How silly!

"It was a stress-induced psychotic break," he said to the tube of toothpaste. The toothpaste, a brand called "SparkleFreshen," did not argue with him, this time anyways. It was a more agreeable audience than Spitfire, who was currently trying to bathe in a shimmering, non-corporeal sunbeam that was cutting through the bathroom steam, and making purring sounds annoyingly. The sunbeam, originating from a crack in the spacetime behind the window curtain, was turning the condensation on the tiles of the bathroom floor into tiny, perfect prisms. "A feedback loop. The accident, the head trauma, the pressure of finals. Turing's face. It's all… explainable." Harvey told himself.

Spitfire paused its ablutions to give him a look that was profoundly unimpressed. It let out a soft *prrrffle* sound, and a tiny, glittering mote of light drifted from its nostril and popped against the light bulb with a faint fizzing sound.

"Right. You're a hallucination. You don't get a vote." Harvey noticed the pizza box that had been knocked out of the overfilled garbage can that had clearly been emptied by Spitfire. "That's too salty for you, Spitfire. I don't think pepperoni is a dietary requirement for dragons."

He walked out of the bathroom, and the world did that thing where it stuttered. For a solid three seconds, the beige hallway carpet of his apartment was replaced with a floor of woven, living roots that pulsed with a soft, subterranean light. The smell of old pizza and Leo's cheap cologne was overwritten by the scent of loam and night-blooming flowers. Then the pills kicked in, the synaptic static rose like a tide, and the roots faded back to worn nylon. The whole process felt less like a cure and more like slapping a strip of duct tape over a warning light on a dashboard that was actively on fire.

A warm rush pulsed through his veins as the medication became effective. He felt nothing again. In the living room, Leo was engaged in his weekly ritual: The Solemn Offering to a new piece of budget-friendly put-together furniture. The partially assembled bookshelf still stood in the center of the room, a monument to frustration. The new addition was to be a small table, so the two of them could play board games together. Leo was circling it, a bag of extra screws in one hand and a rubber mallet in the other, his brow furrowed in concentration.

"I've been approaching this all wrong," Leo announced, not looking up. "It's not just furniture. It's like a relationship. You can't force it, you know? You have to listen to it, give it some time. Understand its needs."

"A bookshelf has needs?" Harvey asked, sinking onto the couch. The cushions felt insubstantial, like he was sitting on a cloud of what cushions should feel like. "I'm not good at relationships anyways, so I shouldn't even chime in."

"See? That's the kind of toxic, results-oriented thinking that doomed my parents' marriage. Yes, a bookshelf has needs. We all have needs. Kinda like your little imaginary dragon friend. And you aren't bad at all relationships, your pet dragon seems to feel loved." Leo half-smiled and tapped the upside-down table gently with the mallet. "There. See? It shifted. It's telling me it's afraid of commitment."

Harvey closed his eyes, but that was worse. The after-image of the dying dragon, a colossal silhouette against a stormy sky, was burned onto the back of his eyelids. The word—*DRAGONBINDER*—echoed not as a sound, but as a seismic event in his psyche. He opened his eyes quickly, focusing on the mundane. A stack of unopened mail on the coffee table. A lonely sock under the TV stand. The stark, red 'F' on the returned draft of his hydroponic farm project, Turing's scrawl beside it: "Structurally unsound. Based on impossible physics. Do better."

He'd tried to explain the way around the impossible physics to Turing during a disastrous office hours visit. He'd talked about harmonic resonance and latent energy fields, which were the most real-world terms he could apply to the glowing runes he saw reinforcing the city's older buildings. Turing had stared at him for a long, silent moment before slowly suggesting he take a medical withdrawal.

A shadow moved outside the window. Not the shadow of a passing bird or a cloud. This was a sleek, serpentine shape, all jagged wings and a long, whip-like tail. It coiled through the air between the apartment blocks, silent and impossibly fast. Harvey flinched, his heart hammering against his ribs. He looked at Leo, who was now trying to soothe the bookshelf by whispering positive affirmations to it. He thought he saw a fleshy dragon creature with mechanical apparatuses coming out of its body. But that seemed even more impossible than his usual delusions.

"Do you see anything weird outside?" Harvey asked, his voice tighter than he intended.

Leo glanced up. "Weirder than when we saw Mrs. Gable taking her pot-bellied pig for a 'walk' in a baby stroller? Not lately. Why?"

"No reason." Harvey lied.

The spectral dragon outside pressed its head against the glass. It had no eyes, just two smoldering pits of ember-like light. It cocked its head, as if studying him. Harvey stared back, frozen. He could feel the heat of its gaze, a dry, ancient heat, like a desert wind. It was really there, wasn't it! Harvey's heart pounded so hard it was painful.

Then Leo's phone rang, blasting a tinny reggae beat. The sound shattered the moment. When Harvey looked back, the creature was gone. Only the gray, drizzling afternoon remained.

That night, sleep was a battleground. The bruise-colored pills pulled him down into a thick, dreamless mud, but something else was pulling him up. He fought it, clinging to the numbness. But the voice of the dragon, Eranthus, was a riptide that jolted his consciousness into a state of waking sleep.

He wasn't in his bed anymore. He was standing on a vast, ashen plain under a sky of churning, purple smoke. In the distance, he saw the creature again. The dragon hung in the air, pinned by half a dozen glowing, crystalline harpoons that dug into its scales. Technomantic runes, glowing the same sterile white as the spear that had struck it, crawled over its body like luminous parasites. Each pulse of light from the runes made the dragon shudder, and a wave of psychic agony washed over the plain.

The booming voice of Eranthus shook Harvey's being. *"They take... grrrrrrrrrrrr... what I am... prrrrrr...* the voice groaned in his mind, a sound of continents shifting... *vakoooooooooommm... They make it... machine... cold...*"

Harvey wanted to cover his ears, but he had no physical presence here. He was just a point of conscious awareness, forced to witness.

"*Grrrrrrrrrrouuu-Must become the dragonbinder... before my song... becomes their static...*"

A fresh harpoon, launched from an unseen source below, slammed into the dragon's chest. It plunged into the creature, tearing through layered scales and sinewed flesh. The death-scream that followed was a silent, universe-ending detonation in Harvey's soul.

• ▬▬▬▬▬ • ▬▬▬▬▬ • ▬▬▬▬▬ •

Harvey woke up gasping, drenched in a cold sweat. The digital clock on his bedside table read 3:17 AM.

For a single, blissful second, there was only the dark, quiet room. Then he saw it. The entire wall opposite his bed was gone. Not broken, just... absent. In its place was the storm-wracked sky of the floating citadel, the rain driving sideways. The black dragon, Eranthus, hung there, immense and terrifyingly close, one vast, pain-filled eye staring directly at him. The eye was a cracked landscape of molten gold and despair. He blinked, and the wall was back. Beige paint. A poster for a band he used to like.

The back and forth was too much to bear. Harvey curled up into a ball and covered himself in his over-sized blanket. It was a winter blanket, thick and heavy. Far too much for this time of year. It was too large, and too warm. But it was something.

He sat there in the dark, waiting for the static to return, for the duct tape of hope to cause one stable universe to hold longer than a moment. He listened to the sound of his own ragged breathing and the distant, fading echo of a dragon's song turning into his own snoring.

4

Everything in this Realm and the Next

Everything in this realm and the next was starting to look less like a coherent system and more like a bad photocopy of two different documents. The new, stronger medication made everything in the "real" world feel muffled and distant, as if he were watching his life through a thick pane of greasy glass. But the fantasy world was now pressing in, sharp and insistent, like a splinter working its way towards his heart.

Harvey now found himself standing on the corner of West Wash and Park Street, a perfectly ordinary intersection in downtown Madison. To anyone else, it was a drab block dominated by a multi-story parking garage, its concrete stained with decades of exhaust fumes. To Harvey, it was the same. The only notable feature was a dusty, perpetually closed park shelter, crammed between a wealthy neighborhood of lakeside homes and a vape shop.

Harvey hopped on his bicycle and rode for several blocks until he reached the city library. The building was a skeletal ruin of cement and glass, and what had once been a library of impossible scale and high class now had dozens of homeless people sleeping on nearby benches. Harvey looked up and saw

29

great, spiraling towers of petrified wood and fused quartz that soared into the sky, their peaks lost in the low-hanging clouds of the Aetherium.

Vines thick as his arm, dripping with bioluminescent sap, crawled over collapsed archways. He saw both at once: the grimy concrete ramp and the grand, shattered staircase; the "My Dog Is Smarter Than Your Honor Student!" bumper sticker on a parked Camry and the elegant, glowing runes carved into the stone above a gaping entrance. A wave of city smell punched Harvey in the face. You know the smell: rotten falafel, cherry-vape-juice, and the ozone-clean scent of a thunderstorm that had just passed.

This place had always been a hot spot, a blurry channel in the broadcast of his life. He remembered many trips here as a child. The library, the museum, the capital, so many things happened downtown. It was the vibrant center of this land that drew people from every direction. They came for cheese, beer and an education. He hadn't come down here much since the accident. It was a remarkably beautiful feeling to take in its splendor, both in the real world and the Aetherium.

"Okay, Harvey," he muttered to himself, his breath misting in the chilly afternoon air. "You're not going in. You're just… observing. Like a scientist. A very, very mentally ill scientist." He gathered the courage to take action and took a step towards the library.

The display window was a jumble of yellowed paperbacks and a faded poster for a local tarot reader. The poster beckoned with an inviting glow. But superimposed over it was the great, dark maw of the library entrance, from which a soft, cool light emanated. He could hear the faint, rhythmic drip-drop plip-plop of water from inside the ruin, a sound that existed in no other world but this one. He was sure of that much.

He pushed the library door open. A bell jingled, a thin, cheap sound. The air inside was thick with the smell of decaying paper and dust. An old man with a spectacularly unkempt white beard was asleep behind the counter, a copy of Zen and the Art of Motorcycle Maintenance splayed open on his chest. But there was another door. A heavy and creaky-looking door made of rune-carved petrified wood that was just to the left of a revolving rack of discounted thrillers. The door appeared to be slightly ajar.

"Don't be an idiot, this is literally how every horror movie starts. Don't go near the creepy door. Stay away from the creepy door." Harvey whispered to himself. He walked over to the thriller rack and picked up a fantasy book. Just what the world needs, another coming of age fantasy tale with dragons. Yikes. No. When he was younger, The Nexus Prince had been his favorite story, he remembered that much. He was older now, more mature, old enough to know he shouldn't waste his time fantasizing about make believe worlds.

He put the paperback down, and a young boy appeared interested in having his turn at the book. "Are you not getting this today?" The boy asked eagerly. "I've seen the animated show, listened to the podcast, and I'm so excited for the movie this summer!"

Harvey sighed. "So, you've experienced the tale on every medium except the one it was actually written on?"

"I'm not the best at reading."

"Fair enough. I think I used to be. I don't remember though." Suddenly it dawned on Harvey that he didn't remember the story of the book at all. He remembered that he read it, but that was all. He couldn't recall any characters, or events that actually happened in the story. How incredibly odd.

He reckoned it wasn't the biggest deal. Aren't those stories all the same anyways? And Harvey felt like the fantasy tropes always got it wrong. In the stories the main character always winds up with a beautiful girl, but Harvey had never even had a conversation with any girl. The dragons were always reliable and didn't smell bad in the stories. The countless hours that Harvey had spent cleaning up dragon waste begged to differ with that notion.

Oh, the accident. That was likely the reason why he couldn't remember the details of his favorite story. It made sense now. Severe head injuries will do that sort of thing. You will remember things, but not that one thing. It's like a giant puzzle at a local nursing home, and one of the residents knocks a few pieces on the floor, which were sadly swept up by the weekend janitor. Those pieces are now gone forever.

He looked at the petrified wood door. The runes along its edge were pulsing with a slow, patient light. Drip-drop. Plip-plop. "Totally normal…" He thought.

He took a step towards it. Then another. He reached out a hand, expecting to feel the solid, grainy wood. His fingers passed through the image, meeting only empty air. He felt like a fool. Of course it wasn't real. He was just a man standing in a dusty library, hallucinating a door.

He let out a shaky breath, half relief, half despair, and turned to leave.

"Most people pick a book," a dry voice said from behind him. "It's generally considered the point of the establishment. Do you need help finding what you are looking for?"

"Oh don't mind my friend, he's just here to meet me!" A strange voice called from behind Harvey.

Harvey spun around. Leaning against a tall, precarious stack of encyclopedias was a young man about his own age, maybe a few years older. He was tall and gaunt, dressed in clothes that looked thrifted from several different centuries: worn corduroy trousers, a surprisingly clean chartreuse velour buttoned up dress- shirt and a long, dark blue velvety cashmere coat that was frayed at the cuffs. His hair was a messy black nest, and a pair of spectacles with translucent lenses were perched on his nose. He was standing while reading a thick, leather-bound volume and looking at Harvey with an expression of profound, academic boredom.

"Who…" Harvey stammered. "I'm sorry, do I know you?"

The man blinked slowly. "Regrettably, yes. I mean-kinda sorta-ish at best? You don't know me, but rather I know you. But water off a camel's snout, what's a guy to do, eh? You are fairly famous, after all. Ugh–Your dimensional flickering is giving me a migraine. It's like watching a strobe light have an existential crisis. And trust me, I know exactly what that looks like.Are you going to actually read anything, or are you just here to vibrate unpleasantly in the Philosophy section?"

Harvey could only stare. The man standing before him looked sort of magical in a way, which made Harvey wonder if he was still in the real world or if he had somehow slipped into Aetherium again. He looked around cautiously.

His tattered suit and stylish choices didn't match Madison, or anything he had yet seen in Nosidam either.

"What do you mean I'm famous? I'm definitely not famous. I'm not even a streamer. I don't care for that sort of thing." Harvey asked, his voice a hoarse whisper.

The man sighed, a long-suffering exhalation. He closed his book with a definitive thump. "Oh, you're famous alright. You can't just phase in and out of different dimensions and think it's nothing special, dear. So–A dragonrider is what you are supposedly. That's what they say, anyways." He half-smiled curiously. "How cliche, huh? You are the talk of the land. But I thought you would be, I don't know– a little more legendary-looking. Or at least taller. I just see a young man before me who looks like he recently lost a fistfight with life. My professional opinion, for what it's worth, is that you look like crap. Let me help. Come on, let's go. Also, is that a pet dragon you have hiding behind you? Hmm, that's odd. I didn't think those existed in your realm." Spitfire purred, puzzled.

He didn't move towards the bookstore's exit. He turned and walked directly towards the petrified wood door that wasn't there. He didn't open it. He simply… phased through it, his form shimmering for a split second before he vanished.

Harvey stood frozen, his heart trying to punch its way out of his rib cage. The sleeping man at the counter snored once, loudly. The bell on the door jingled as a woman entered, heading straight for the romance section. That's where the real money is, romance. Harvey made a mental note to himself, in case he ever would decide to become a writer.

The stranger he had just met had a type of energy that had comforted him greatly, and he found himself longing to follow the man. Perhaps he could give him more answers he was looking for.

"Come on then Harvey, we haven't got all day! Keep those feet movin' not dragon—get it?" Linus always felt silly when he needed to explain his bad pun jokes, but they brought him so much joy. And occasionally, a glimmer of a smile would trace across a stranger's face at his dark humor as well, (but that was rare, indeed).

He looked at the space where the gaunt man had disappeared. He looked at the mundane, dusty library. Then, taking a breath that felt like his first in weeks, Harvey took a step forward, through the space where the door wasn't, and into the ethereal realm of Aetherium.

5

The Beguiled Whispers of Forgotten Loves

The Grand Crystal Treasury didn't just hold countless old books; it held countless old books that were likely considered minor acts of heresy in some worlds, and were now contemplating their life choices themselves. (Yes, books can feel remorse, just ask one).

The books held tales of guilt, vellum, and the beguiled whispers of forgotten loves. The books were not made of paper parchment, but of sheer, harnessed crystal. The pages contained multitudes of images, words, sounds, stories, emotions. Think 8k, but about one hundred times more clear.

Harvey stood just inside the petrified-wood door—which was now very, very solid behind him—and tried to get his bearings. The place was a cathedral of lost knowledge. Shelves carved from living crystals soared into a gloom punctuated by floating, self-contained globes of light that drifted like lazy fireflies. Staircases spiraled off into nothingness, and the floor was a mosaic of a star chart for constellations that had died out millennia ago.

"Well hey, glad you decided to join. I'm Linus, by the way. Linus Malcolm

Bordeaux the III, to be precise.. As in, I'm bored'o your drama. Or what would likely happen if you combined a pig with cookie dough, boar dough. Or just Bordeaux." The gaunt man was already several paces ahead, not bothering to check if Harvey was keeping up. He walked with the weary slouch of a man on his way to a job he'd been working for three hundred years too long.

"So," Harvey said, his voice echoing in the vast space. "What's your deal, anyways? Are you… a… librarian or something?"

Linus paused by a desk that was a single slab of polished obsidian, piled high with scrolls. He took off a pair of spectacles with perfectly intact lenses, and threw them onto the ground, replacing them with a pair he pulled out of his coat pocket that had cracked and smeared glass. He eagerly grinned at the vision produced by this new pair.

"Ah yes, now I see. Oh, you asked a question. Sorry. I am many things! A scientist, a gardener. A librarian, yes. I believe that's what it's called in this world. I think the official title is Grand Archivist VI. I also play the flute a wee bit. Since we are now dear friends, you should also know that my favorite color is purple. Indigo, to be precise."

Harvey smiled a half-hearted smile, not sure if he should entertain a friendship so quickly obtained.

Linus corrected, his tone implying there was a vast difference between the two professions. "I hope to someday be certified to be a level VII someday, but honestly who can afford to invest in themselves in this economy. A librarian helps you find books on plumbing. An Archivist prevents the fundamental concepts of 'wet' and 'pipe' from unraveling and leaking into the astral plane. The pay is comparable, but the stakes are marginally higher. One saves you money from not having to buy all the books you want to read, one may hold the power to save all of existence on a routine basis."

He began walking again, and Harvey hurried to keep up, his sneakers squeaking on the star-chart floor. "Sounds impressive. And can I ask– do you–do you know what I am?"

"I know you're some kind of Nexus Walker, that's for sure. Albeit, a messy one. You trail bits of your reality around you like a toddler with a leaky jam sandwich. Some may find it academically fascinating, however others with class (such as me) may find such irresponsibility personally revolting. I believe the phrase here from your world would be 'Can't you get a grip dude?'"

"I don't think so. I think the whole surfer lingo stopped being colloquial in the 90s, actually." Harvey said.

He gestured vaguely at Harvey. "So, a Nexus Walker and pompous ass. Interesting mix indeed! That is curious, honestly. Usually it's the disciplined mystics or wise sages that fall through, they don't last long though. So how did you get your powers? Psychedelic adventurer? Did someone slip you the ol' shiny blue tea on a safari? On a wholly separate note, the static from your world is giving me a low-grade psychic sunburn. Do you people ever just... switch off?"

"We have a thing called video games. Sometimes I switch those off, but I try to avoid it if I'm being honest."

Linus shot him a look that was almost, but not quite, appreciative. "Noted."

"And I'm not a mystic or a monk or anything like that, sorry to disappoint you. I'm just a normal college kid. Well, just a college kid I guess. Maybe not so normal."

Linus smirked. "Well, no dragon binder is normal. They are beings that can channel communication with dragons, after all. I've just never heard of one like you before."

They arrived at a smaller, circular chamber dominated by a large, wooden table that was so covered in carvings and inlays it looked like a map of a schizophrenic's nervous system. Linus swept a pile of delicate metal tools and copper wiring onto a nearby chair with a practiced, careless motion.

"Sit dear prince," he commanded, pointing to a stool. "Before you faint. You appear to have the pallor of unleavened dough."

Harvey sat. The weight of the last few weeks, the sleepless nights, the chemical fog of the pills, all crashed down on him at once. He put his head in his hands. "People think I'm crazy. My professors, my doctor, even my roommate... I was starting to think they were right."

"Well, they're not right," Linus said, his voice losing some of its abrasive edge. He leaned against the table, crossing his arms. "They're just...

monochromatic. They can only perceive one frequency of existence. You, through a combination of genetic fluke, head trauma, and what I can only assume was a profoundly interesting childhood, can perceive two. Congratulations. It's a lousy gift, but it's yours."

"The dragon," Harvey said, looking up. "Eranthus. It's… talking to me. In my head."

"Hmm, yes. He's dying unfortunately. Beings of immense power tend to make a lot of psychic noise when that happens. Think of a whale song, if the whale was the size of a mountain and its song was the conceptual framework for 'fire.'" Linus pushed his glasses up his nose. "And you're not just hearing it. He thinks you're the one he's calling for, so you're feeling it too. The call of the dragonbinder."

The word hung in the air between them, no longer a terrifying accusation, but a job title. A profoundly unwanted one.

"I can't bind a dragon. I can barely bind my own shoelaces some mornings."

"It's a misnomer," Linus said, waving a dismissive hand. "A crude translation from a language that died out when your world's continents were still holding hands. It's not about binding, not in the sense of chains. It's about… resonance. Harmony. A dragonbinder doesn't control a dragon. He… tunes to it, and he tunes it to himself. I always thought a different name would be appropriate, honestly. Because the dragonbinder is the one binding themselves in their emotions, it really has very little to do with the dragons themselves. A dragonbinder amplifies its connection to the fundamental forces of everything. He's a living focusing lens."

"For what?"

"For balance, ideally" a new voice said, sharp and cold as a shard of glass. "But the prophecies typically tell of dragonbinders bringing destruction, not balance.

Kael emerged from between two towering shelves, her leather armor silently rubbing against the crystal. She looked at Harvey with the same simmering distrust he remembered from when she shoved him from one realm to the next. "The dragonbinder maintains the equilibrium between the Aetherium and the… other place." She said 'other place' the way someone might say 'sewage treatment plant.'

"You mean Earth," Harvey offered.

"I know your world's name. And I know your name too, Harvey Chandler. You are the one the prophecies spoke of. Everyone in Aetherium has heard of you, but we just didn't think you would come through in our time. I have come to apologize for our last encounter, and to ask you to have mercy on our world."

A moment of awkward silence ensued, as the three adventurers glanced at one another, each with a distrusting glare.

Harvey backed himself up, maintaining a distance from Kael, afraid she would shove him again. Her eyes glared at him, like daggers.

"Kael, you don't need to be afraid of me. We don't even know if I'm the dragonbinder."

Kael glanced down at Spitfire, shrugging accusingly.

"Yeah, I guess there's that… Kind of a give away as to your true destiny when it follows you around everywhere like a lost puppy dog." Linus cleared his throat. "As I was explaining before the one-woman siege engine arrived, the balance–. The balance is failing. Turing's technomancy is like a parasite. It doesn't create; it converts. It's turning the Aetherium's magic into a sterile, programmable energy. And it's using Eranthus as the primary power source."

"So we take out Eranthus?," Harvey said, the words feeling absurd even as he said them.

"Why are you quick to choose that option." Kael said, her flinty eyes fixed on him. "Not only do we lack the power to *take out* a dragon, our world is powered by the dragons. If we take one out, we would be causing catastrophic loss, the level of which cannot possibly be fathomed. Whenever a dragon dies, there is always a dragon to take its place. You can't just kill one, it disrupts the whole order of everything. And the technomancy has already gone too far. Severing the connection now would kill Eranthus instantly and release a cataclysm of unstable energy that could potentially shred both our worlds. It would be like trying to stop a dam from breaking by blowing up the reservoir."

"Lovely imagery," Linus muttered. "So, we don't unplug him, we install a better surge protector." He turned back to Harvey. "As an experienced archivist, I'll have you know I've done my share of reading! Reading crystals of course, I'm not a wild animal. I recall that legend speaks of an artifact called the Heartstone. It's said to be a crystallized fragment of the first dragon's heart. It can amplify a true dragonbinder's power exponentially. With it, you could theoretically… re-calibrate the connection. Purge Turing's influence from Eranthus and reinforce the barrier between our worlds. Permanently. I'm just making an educated guess here, of course."

Harvey stared at him. "Wait—you're talking about a quest. A fantasy quest! With a magical MacGuffin? This is literally the plot for every fantasy story ever written. Oh, I'm definitely in!" For the longest time in recent memory, Harvey felt a surge of excitement. He always loved role-playing games. This would be like the penultimate LARPing adventure.

"Well, I for one would argue that is simply not possible, because this story has me in it as a central character. What more could any reader want? That makes it special, unique, likely to fly off the shelves! So, I'm talking about a complex, inter dimensional engineering problem with a very high probability of failure," Linus corrected. "But yes, if you need to dumb it down for your own primate brain to process, sure, it's a quest like all the others."

"And do you know where this Heartstone is?" Harvey asked.

Linus smiled, a thin, brittle expression that held no warmth. "I have a theory. The archival texts are infuriatingly vague, written by poets who valued a good rhyme over useful information. (See introduction, page 1).

Kael stepped forward. "The Crystal Archives is where it is located."

"Not to sour the mood, but why should we trust you exactly? You attacked me last time." Harvey proclaimed.

"Again, I've had some time to think. I know the prophecies. But I also see what is happening with this evil technology. I just want to save my world" Kael said, tapping the table. "So you might be able to find the Archives on your own, but you will need my help to get through to find the Heartstone. She pointed a long, pale finger downwards towards the large crossbow hanging conveniently over her shoulder. "It's beneath your city. In the places your people buried and forgot. Your abandoned tunnels."

Harvey felt a cold knot tighten in his stomach. The idea was insane. It was also the first thing that had made a terrible, twisted kind of sense in weeks. He wasn't just a passive victim of his visions anymore. He was being given a map. A stupid, dangerous, possibly imaginary map, but a map nonetheless.

He looked from Linus's weary, intellectual face to Kael's hardened, warrior's scowl. He was just a student who'd just failed an important exam, teaming up with a sarcastic archivist, scientist librarian of sorts and a woman who probably sharpened her crossbow bolts with her teeth to find a magical rock in a surely haunted subway system to save a dragon and two realities.

"Okay," Harvey said, his voice quiet but steady. "Let's work together to do this. So how do we start?"

Linus's brittle smile widened just a fraction. "Now that's a good question. We start by doing what you do best. We start by looking at something everyone else sees... and seeing something else entirely."

II

Part Two

These Rocks are Made for Singin'

6

The Caves of Singing Crystal

The entrance to the Caves of Singing Crystal led to the Grand Crystal Treasury. From the platform of the abandoned tunnels below the university station, was a jagged crack in the old, lime-stained tile wall. To Harvey, it was also a grand, arched opening veined with pulsating amethyst and emitting a low, resonant hum that felt like it was cleaning his teeth from the inside out.

"The acoustics in there are supposed to be phenomenal. Who wants to start a rock band?" Linus joked, peering into the darkness. He was holding a small, ornate brass device that clicked and whirred, measuring something Harvey's own world didn't have a name for. "It's said the crystals record every sound ever made within them. If you listen closely, you can hear the philosophical debates of rocks from the last ice age."

"Fascinating," Kael muttered, notching a bolt into her crossbow. The weapon looked profoundly anachronistic in the grimy subway tunnel. "I don't really care about the sounds of the past right now. I'm more concerned with what might be making new sounds. Like the sound of something with too many teeth."

Harvey stood between them, feeling the now-familiar dual perception like a suit he'd reluctantly learned to wear. The real world was a graffiti-covered, damp, and depressing tomb for forgotten transit. The Aetherium layer was a breathtaking geode of impossible scale. Rusty train tracks were also a path of polished river stones that glowed with soft internal light. The puddle of questionable liquid near his foot was also a tiny, perfectly clear pool holding a single, luminescent lily.

"This used to be part of the underground railroad. And there's legends about a guy that lives down here. I think his name was Bob or something." Harvey said, squinting. He'd been using his sight all morning, looking for the tell-tale glitching static of Turing's technomancy. He saw only the pristine, magical beauty of the caves. "It's... clean here. Really clean. Which is surprising considering we are underground."

"That's what worries me," Linus said, tucking his device away. "In my experience, places of great power are usually defended by things with a lot of venom and a bad attitude. This is like finding a vault door wide open with a sign that says 'Free Gold, Please Take Some.' It's either a miracle or a colossally bad idea. I tend to believe it is more likely the latter."

"Love your optimism," Kael said, and without another word, she stepped through the archway, her form swallowed by the deeper shadows of both realities. "I'm still not even sure why I'm helping you, honestly. But if you truly are the dragonbinder, you can fix things, make Eranthus better again. Then hopefully you will just get out of here. I think your people have done enough damage."

"Hey, don't compare me to Turing, please. I don't even know the guy. Well, okay I guess I know him but only in an academic setting, which doesn't really count."

The inside of the cave was a cathedral of sound and light. Massive crystals, like faceted blue topaz the size of redwoods, thrust from the floor and ceiling. The hum was everywhere, causing a physical pressure. As they walked, Harvey's sneakers on the gritty concrete were accompanied by the soft chime of his teammates' boots on the resonant stone. He could hear faint, ghostly echoes—the drip of water, a fragment of whispered song, the distant roar of what might have been a prehistoric beast.

"If my memory serves me right, the texts said the Heartstone would be here somewhere. It's been so long since I read that codex, though." Linus whispered, his voice barely disturbing the acoustic sanctity. "It's been sooooo long" he sang out to text the reverberation. His voice trailed on and on for what sounded like forever.

"Shh," Kael cautioned. "We don't want any visitors."

"It's hard to be silent in a world made entirely of sound, you know. It's so exciting! That's the thing about the Aetherium. Every crystal holds the memories of all who came before us. Most people just can't hear the sound, even most of the people who live here are oblivious to it!" Linus twirled around in a circle daintily like an absolute madman.

Harvey was amused by the thought of sound as memory. "So what's the point then, of having the memories recorded by the crystals if nobody can even hear it. I guess I just don't understand."

"Oh Harvey, there is every reason. The stories of old cannot truly ever be lost, they live inside of us all. There are always people who try to erase history, that happens in each world. But the purpose of the sound isn't to be recognized or accepted for some universal, objective truth. Sometimes the act of singing is what it's all about! Don't tell me your world still writes on stone tablets?"

"Well, we have books. Paperbacks. And hardcovers. And e Books are a thing now too. It's like a digital copy of a book where you can read it on a screen like a tablet. Libraries with books. And movies. We do have songs too, but we don't have crystals like this. Not that I know of, anyways."

"Oh egad, how absolutely primitive. I think we moved past that eons ago here in the Aetherium. At least you've moved beyond cave painting though, so I guess some progress is better than nothing. So, e books. You write on fancy stone tablets. Got it." Linus smirked.

They followed a descending path, the air growing colder. The techno-color brilliance of the crystals began to feel oppressive, like being inside a giant, functioning circuit board. Harvey's headache, a constant companion since the car accident, began to sharpen from a dull throb into a precise, drilling pain behind his eyes.

Ahead of them they saw a half-circle desk, with a slight old woman. Her skin was a very pallid blue, and she appeared to be an impossibly ancient librarian. Her skin had wrinkled to the point that the wrinkles took on a life of their own, with deep canyon pits into her flesh, and rising ridges. "Visitors? Oh—my word, let me see if I have any cookies for you. Can't do reading without cookies, now can we? Oh, I'm getting ahead of myself now aren't I? Well hello there! I'm Magpie Maggie. Come to search for something? Oh, I don't remember feeling this excited for quite a while! You are the first visitors in quite a while. What is it you seek, hmm? Oh?" Her words came out slow and thought out.

"We are looking for the heartstone." Harvey proclaimed. "Can you tell us where to find it?"

Magpie Maggie wore a patchwork dress made of old robes torn and stitched together from iniquity. Her voice was cracking and jagged, and Harvey wondered when the last time was that she had used it for any reason. "Heartstone? Oh, you must mean the heart that is made of stone. I vaguely remember the tale. Oh, you won't find that here. Nope. Oh? Do you even know what to do when you find the it, oh?"

"We are trying to save Eranthus the dragon."

"Ohhhh." Magpie Maggie seemed to have an aha moment. "Is that what all the ruckus has been about? Well, why didn't you say so, oh? Eranthus is a dear old friend of all in the Aetherium, yes he is. But the heartstone is just a story, boy. Everything is just a story. Do you get it now? So, you don't need to find a stone, you are the stone."

Harvey looked back and forth to Kael and Linus. They all seemed equally puzzled. "I don't understand."

A shiny worm appeared next to Magpie Maggie and whispered in a silly old English voice. Harvey was sure they were saying something, but it just sounded like *"Wishinabakinahabina."* The decibel range of the worm was just too low for his human ears to perceive.

"Oh? This is that boy? Well, I'll be!" Magpie Maggie stood up and pointed to a door behind them. "Through that door you go, you'll find your answers there."

The three adventurers entered a vast, circular chamber. In the center, on a natural pedestal of stone, it rested. There it was, the Heartstone. It was a deep, blood-red crystal, about the size of a human heart, and it pulsed with a slow, inviting light. It was truly gorgeous, perhaps the most beautiful thing Harvey had ever seen. It looked... friendly.

"See?" Harvey said, a wave of relief washing over him. "I knew it was real. It's the heartstone." He did wonder why she had made the comment about it not being real, and about him being the heartstone.

Linus didn't move. He was staring at the stone, his brow furrowed. "That's... it?"

"It matches the descriptions," Kael said, though she kept her crossbow raised, scanning the shadows between the crystals.

"Exactly," Linus said, his voice tight. "It matches them a little too well. He pulled out a single spectacle and put it under one eye, tossing the other glasses away like they meant nothing. "Pulsating crimson core, facets of captured starlight. It's like someone read a poem about it and then built a prop. Real artifacts of power tend to be... messier. They have cracks. Flaws. This looks like it was manufactured last Tuesday. I have doubts about its authenticity."

Before Harvey could process this, a new sound joined the hum of the caves. A sound like a hundred locusts made of metal, skittering and scraping. From behind every major crystal, sleek, canine-like robotic constructs emerged. They had six legs of articulated chrome, bodies of brushed steel, and heads that were single, glowing red camera lenses. They moved with a jerky, entomological precision that was utterly alien to both worlds.

"I've seen these things before," Kael spat, raising her crossbow. "Turing's dragonets."

"It's a trap. A profoundly obvious one," Linus said, grabbing Harvey's arm. "We need to leave. Now."

But Harvey was frozen, his eyes locked on the Heartstone. It was pulsing faster now, in time with his heartbeat. A thin, almost invisible beam of white light connected it to his chest. He could feel it pulling at him, not physically, but deeper. It was tapping into the warm, humming connection he felt to

Spitfire, to the moss on his walls, to the dying song of Eranthus. It felt like a siphon starting its work.

"I… I can't move," he gasped. The drilling pain in his head became an ice pick.

The metal hounds didn't attack. They simply formed a silent, clicking circle around the chamber, their red lenses watching.

A figure stepped out from behind the largest crystal. He wasn't a grizzled warlord or a robed wizard. He was a man in an impeccably tailored gray suit, looking like he'd just stepped out of a board meeting. He was clean-shaven, with short, neat hair and wore glasses with thin, silver frames. The only thing that was off were his gloves, made of a strange, coppery mesh that shimmered with the same sterile white energy as the harpoons that pierced Eranthus.

"You must be Dr. Turing," Linus said, his voice dripping with academic disdain. "The dress code for 'multiverse domination' is more business casual than I anticipated. Here I was expecting a evil cape and hood, but you sure look dashing, I must say."

Turing ignored him. His eyes, a calm and calculating blue, were fixed on Harvey.

"Harvey Chandler, my annoying student. Well, where's your dragon?" Turing asked, as he looked around confused. His voice was pleasant, reasonable. "The dragonbinder is supposed to have a dragon, is he not? Oh, Harvey, you truly are a disappointment."

"You were a crappy professor anyways. None of the students learned anything from you. You copied and pasted your feedback that you gave us." Harvey managed to grit out, the siphon's pull growing stronger. He felt a part of himself, the part that could feel Spitfire's warmth, starting to go numb.

"The boy that can speak to dragons, and here you are whining about my grading criteria. You make quite the dragonbinder, my boy. Ha! I guess you have failed at that, just like you fail at school. How predictable. All you young people are the same. Good thing I don't need you to succeed in order to get what I want."

Linus stepped forward. "What is it that you want?"

"Oh, the prophecy was just a user manual," Turing corrected gently. "You see, I couldn't be the dragonbinder myself, and I kept asking myself how to get the power from the dragonbinder. Such a messy, metaphysical concept. Who knows if it even exists honestly, sounds silly. All that empathy. That connection. And all I needed was the source code." He reached forward and grabbed the heartstone in his gloved hand, and it glowed brighter. The beam connecting it to Harvey solidified into a cord of blinding white light. "And you were kind enough to deliver it to my server farm, so thank you for that."

The hearthstone wasn't an actual physical thing. It was Harvey's heart.

Harvey screamed. It wasn't a scream of pain, but of loss. It was the feeling of a sense being surgically removed. The vibrant colors of the Aetherium layer in the cave flickered, grayed out, and then stabilized, but now felt distant, muted, like a song played on a cheap radio.

"What are you doing to him?" Kael snarled, firing her crossbow. The bolt shattered harmlessly against an invisible energy field around Turing.

"Harvesting," Turing said, his tone still conversational. "Don't worry, he'll be just fine. I'm just taking a small, foundational fragment. Enough to bootstrap the process. My Aetherblade won't need a living dragon's heart. It will have a core powered by purified dragonbinding potential. A perfect, logical, obedient engine. No messy songs. No pesky emotions. Just pure, calculable power."

With a final, wrenching sensation, the connection severed. The fake Heartstone went dark, now just a lump of red glass. The beam vanished. Harvey collapsed to his knees, gasping. The world hadn't vanished, but a crucial channel had been switched off. The silence in his head was deafening.

"A worthwhile trade," Turing said, adjusting his cuff links. "A sliver of your potential for the knowledge that you have already lost. Do try to hold on to the rest. I may be needing it later."

He gave a slight, polite nod, and then he and his metal hounds simply dissolved into a shower of static and were gone.

The caves were silent, save for the hum of the crystals and Harvey's ragged breathing. Linus rushed to his side.

"Harvey? Talk to me. What did he take?"

Harvey looked up, his vision swimming. He could still see the crystals, but they were just pretty rocks now. The glow was aesthetic, not alive. He couldn't hear the song anymore. The background music that he had heard his whole life, just gone.

"He took something from me," Harvey whispered, the truth of it hollowing him out. "I am not even sure what it was exactly, but something feels different."

7

Shameless, Future Self-Promotion

Reader, do you find yourself enjoying "The Nexus Prince?"

Be sure to tell your friend, your friend's friend, and perhaps a family member if you are still on speaking terms with them. If you do not have friends or a family, you can always share your opinions with a nearby clump of sentient moss. They are always listening, and they care about you too, rest assured!

Be sure to listen to The Nexus Prince Audiobook, coming soon. Also be sure to check out the comic, animated television series and motion picture event, coming much less soon, if ever at all.

Don't forget to buy a The Nexus Prince themed t-shirt, and eat The Nexus Prince frozen pizzas (gluten free varieties available, of course). You can find The Nexus Prince frozen pizzas available wherever you buy frozen pizzas.

And most importantly, be sure to join The Nexus Prince fan club, on The Nexus Prince app, which requires you to complete six and a half step verification. And don't worry, if you forget your password, or your pass code, or any of the several thousand useless steps we make you go through, it's okay! You will still be a fan, and you will still find yourself obsessed with The Nexus Prince, and we will still be more than happy to take your hard earned dollars from you.

And if you have The Nexus Prince in paperback, hard cover, audio book, and are wearing the t-shirt whilst you await the arrival on the cinematic big screen, why not purchase some The Nexus Prince flavored air you can sniff while you wait? Smells like dragon's breath, guaranteed!

And don't forget, every single step of the way will require two-step verification. You can't build a bright-lit station in your nation without verified verification, everybody knows that.

In a world where everything is an advertisement, and sometimes even an advertisement for an advertisement, where there are viral videos of people watching viral videos, what pray tell is next? Products that sell products that sell products?

How many levels deep does this go?

Until we are 6 and a half feet under, none of us will know.

But the algorithms grow, and the lawnmowers mow, as is reaped what is sown, and mysteries unknown. We are all, each one of us alone, when the ol' bell tolls, 'for the beckoner's pulse'a the other side of Tulsa, Velveteen ulcer.

8

To the Sewers, We Traverse!

The world had gone flat.

Back in his apartment, Harvey stared at the wall where Steve, the bioluminescent moss usually pulsed with a melancholic blue. Now, it was just a wall. Beige paint. A hairline crack he'd never noticed before. The silence in his head was a physical presence, a wad of cotton stuffed into the part of his mind that used to hear the hum of the universe. He felt… monolingual. Or something.

Which was odd, because Harvey could actually speak multiple languages. English, French, Spanish, German, and a very small amount of colloquial Thai. He had been indecisive on which language he should learn, so he just dabbled a bit in them all. He wasn't fluent in any of them other than English, but he could understand enough, especially since he was by no means a world traveler. Dimension jumper, apparently. But his passport was barren.

The French word for a toy is jouet. It would be spielzeug in German. He couldn't remember what it would be in Spanish or Thai. Spitfire was a plush toy again. A dumb, inanimate collection of polyester stuffing and plastic pellets. Harvey picked it up. The fabric was cool and inert. He didn't feel the

56

familiar warmth, the subtle thrum of a miniature star contained within. He tossed it onto the couch, and it landed like a pathetic lump. He was sure the dragon had been real just moments ago.

"It's like I've gone deaf in one ear," he said to the empty room. His voice sounded too loud. "Ugh."

Leo poked his head out of his bedroom. "You say something? Also, have you seen my lucky socket wrench? I've been looking for it for hours."

"No," Harvey said, not specifying which question he was answering.

"Right. Well, if you see it, let me know please. Also, hi. Hope you're having a good afternoon." Leo's head disappeared.

Harvey's phone, a brick of mundane technology, buzzed. A text from an unknown number.

I'm on campus. Study hall. You know the one. Bring coffee. The kind from your world that tastes bitter. Oh, also make sure it's warm. How could anyone drink anything cold at a time like this? -Linus.

The study hall was a forgotten alcove in the back of the university's Asian Art department, a room that smelled of dust, rock samples, and the profound disappointment of students who had mistaken "Earth Sciences" for an easy credit. To Harvey, it had once been a vibrant modernized scriptorium where floating quills copied star-charts onto vellum made of solidified moonlight. Now, it was just a dusty alcove again.

There were several study halls on campus. Some were busy hot spots, with convenient cafes, coffee shops and specialized vending machines. Some were so busy you needed to wait in a line until a seat would open up. Some were quiet study spaces, where talking of any kind was not allowed, and you could hear the frustrated breathing patterns of nervous students who had put off their project until the last minute and now were panicked.

Linus was already there, hunched over a workbench covered in a bizarre assortment of items: a cracked smartphone connected by copper wires to a piece of amethyst, a half-eaten bag of potato chips, and several open books with titles like "Ontological Paradoxes in a Quasi-Quantum Framework" and "For Dummies: Basic Thermodynamic Principles."

"How did you know this place?" Harvey inquired.

"You're late," Linus said without looking up. He tapped the smartphone screen, which was displaying a waveform analyzer. "I know of many places, dear friend. And you didn't bring coffee? The foundation of our entire plan is crumbling."

"He took it from me, Linus,"

"The coffee? Likely excuse, Harv."

"No, not the coffee. The connection I had to my dragon." Harvey said, slumping into a rickety wooden chair. "I can't… feel it anymore. I can't feel Spitfire. It's all just… stuff now. But why can I still see you here then?"

Linus finally looked at him, pushing his glasses up his nose. "That is puzzling, honestly. But it's a neat trick for sure! As far as what happened to you; some kind of traumatic psychic amputation. Very dramatic, no doubt. So, I'm conducting a field test. Hold still." He gestured to the smartphone-amethyst contraption. "This is measuring the ambient thaumic field around you. Before Turing's little theft, you were reading at a steady 7.3 kilothaums. You're now fluctuating between 6.1 and 6.4. Turing may have taken a chunk, but not the whole pie."

"A chunk of what?"

"Your potential. The raw, unfocused ability to interface with the Aetherium's dragons. Think of it as him stealing your… artistic talent. You can still see the colors, but you can't paint the masterpiece."

"So what's the point?" Harvey gestured around the dusty room. "He's building his mechanized dragon. I'm… diminished. We lost before the battle even began."

"Well—we lost Plan A," Linus corrected, turning back to his contraption. "Plan A was elegant. Use a legendary artifact to perform a system-wide harmonic re-calibration. It was the equivalent of a perfectly written piece of software. Plan A is now a smoking crater." He picked up a potato chip, examined it and flipped it upside down so that the side with the most seasoning would be the one to touch his tongue, and ate it. "So we move to Plan B."

"Which is?"

"Plan B is messy. Plan B is throwing a monkey wrench into the cogs of the machine and hoping the resulting explosion kills the other guy and not us." Linus wiped his fingers on his trousers. "Spitfire."

Harvey stared at him. "Spitfire my pet dragon? But he's not even here anymore."

"Precisely. Turing stole a fragment of your potential. His power is a copy. A bootleg. It's logical, sterile, and perfect for running a machine. But a living dragon… that's not a machine. It's a chaotic, beautiful, emotional mess of biology and magic. His stolen, sterile power might not be able to interface with it. A live dragon could be an immune system response he can't counter."

"I don't follow your logic. Turning has already proven he can do just that, he can interface directly with dragons."

"Apologies. My brain stopped working for a moment there. It happens once in a while. We need to worry about Spitfire for sure then! There's a place called The Sundering Peak where the dragons go to rest. All dragons go there at some point. It's kind of like a save point for them, a place to reset their thaumic energy. That's likely where Spitfire will be." Linus gave him that brittle smile. "It's a perilous journey, but it's the only plan we have that doesn't involve waiting for him to finish building his doomsday weapon. We go to the Sundering Peak. We find your little buddy, Spitfire. And then we see if there's enough of the ol' 'music' left in you to wake it up."

The Sundering Peak existed atop jagged, ice covered mountains in the Aetherium. Ironically, the journey to get there started in a much different location in the real world.

"Gather your courage, Harvey. This will be an uphill journey, and will likely be a slow, arduous descent through a landscape that will feel like hitting a raw nerve. To the sewers we traverse!"

A puzzled look painted Harvey's face. "The–sewers?

They started in the real world, in the storm drains on the city's outskirts. Linus, to Harvey's surprise, moved through the dripping concrete tunnels with a grim familiarity, his long coat occasionally snagging on rusted rebar.

"You spend a lot of time in sewers?" Harvey asked, his voice echoing.

"Dimensional weak points often coincide with places your society flushes away and forgets," Linus replied, sidestepping a suspiciously green puddle.

"Libraries, Museums, etc. Newer additions are churches and movie theaters, believe it or not. Anyways, the sewers may not be glamorous, but the rent is affordable here, which is a rare find in Madison."

As they walked, the Aetherium layer began to superimpose itself. The concrete tunnel walls became veined with raw, unrefined magic, a shimmering, oily rainbow slick that pulsed with a dangerous energy. The air grew thick and heavy. This wasn't the pristine beauty of the Crystal Caves or the ordered majesty of the Grand Crystal Archives. This was the back end. The server room of reality, full of exposed wiring and primal, unformulated power.

"Don't touch the walls," Linus warned, his usual sarcasm replaced by a sharp tension. "That's raw chaos. It won't kill you, but it might rewrite your personal history so that you were always a devoted fan of polka music."

They navigated a labyrinth of these sewage bleeding, unstable passages. At one point, the path ahead was blocked by a churning vortex of conflicting realities—a shimmering curtain where the laws of physics seemed to be having a vehement argument. Linus spent twenty minutes carefully calibrating his brass device, muttering about "recalcitrant entropy," before finding a safe path around it.

Through their journey, Harvey felt nothing. Even seeing some elements of the Aetherium was just–different than before. He could see the remnants of the magical realm, but he could no longer feel them. The raw chaos should have been a symphony of terror. It was just… a light show. A silent, dangerous light show. The numbness overwhelming him felt like a cage. He imagined this is what a wild caught bird would experience on their first day at the pet shop.

After what felt like (and probably was) hours, they emerged into a cavern so vast the ceiling was lost in a perpetual thunderhead. This was the Sundering Peak. It wasn't a mountain, but the shattered core of a forgotten world, a jagged spire of black rock floating in a void of swirling, color-drained mist. The center of the peak was nestled in a cradle of petrified dragon bones.

Harvey wondered how the mountain tops could be covered in white shimmering ice sheets if they were underground. Then he quickly realized he should not be attempting to apply logic to physics in a magical realm. It didn't make sense, so here it would.

They followed a path that had been paved from previous travelers. Some of it was sandy, some a muddy loam. Some had boards nailed into the ground, forging a makeshift road.

They reached a small cliff that would require climbing. Linus jumped to the top and reached down to pull Harvey up.

"Thank you." Harvey said.

"That's what friends are for." Linus winked at him.

Were they friends? They hadn't known each other that long, after all. But yes, Harvey did feel a sort of camaraderie with Linus that felt strange, alien. He didn't have many friends in the real world. He had a roommate, but he was fairly certain his roommate was more annoyed with him than enjoying his company.

Harvey decided to ask for confirmation? "Are we really friends?"

Linus smiled, catching his breath as they began walking again. "I am certain that we are. If you are indeed the dragonbinder, I have spent my life studying about you. From what I've gathered so far, I may even know you better than you know yourself."

Harvey smiled a big, genuine smile. He couldn't remember the last time he had an actual friend. Did he ever have one before? He wasn't sure. He had made many acquaintances, of course. Dave at the video game store, Jim at the pizzeria, a few of his many foster parents had occasionally had nice things to say when he was younger. But someone to actually call a friend, he couldn't recall ever having one of those.

Perhaps it was because he was shy, always unsure of what to say or how to act. He never had the most impressive clothing, he didn't like popular music, he didn't know how to dance. Harvey was counter-culture long before it was cool.

Harvey felt like a forever foster child, always searching for that sense of belonging and comfort. He had never found it, so he would just create it for himself in his own mind. He did that often, living in his own little world, shut out from reality whenever possible. A good book. A bad book. A movie, or sometimes a movie marathon. A video game, or a video game competition.

Anything to dull the loneliness, and help him to forget who he was. Who he felt he was, anyways. He was worried that someday he might become a druggie, he had all the telltale dispositions in place to be a raging addict, but he was simultaneously too scared to try anything harder than soda pop. He figured life was already hard enough, why add any more suffering to it?

"Can I tell you something?" Harvey asked.

"Of course mate, what's up?"

"I just wanted to let you know, I haven't had many friends before so I may not be good at it. So, sorry about that."

Linus stopped walking and looked Harvey directly in his eyes. "Nonsense, Harvey. Do not ever apologize for who you are. Do you hear me? I am happy to be your friend, and you will have many, many friends in life. Things are not always what they seem. You may feel a certain way, but that doesn't mean it's true. Do you understand?" Linus put his hand on Harvey's shoulder. "I think you're doing a great job, whether you are the dragonbinder or not."

"Thank you." Harvey said. It then dawned on him that neither of them had mentioned Kael. "Should we try to find Kael too?"

"The leather-clad warrior? She is fine. I'm already ahead of you. I asked her to meet us and provided her with a meeting spot up ahead. She's probably hunting a large land animal as we speak."

The two hiked further and Harvey could feel his legs beginning to feel like wobbly jello. "I don't know how much longer I can walk." He muttered, feeling his feet go tingly numb with exhaustion.

"There!" Linus pointed to the right. In the distance they saw Kael's shadow, hunched over something. Harvey squinted and saw that it was Spitfire. He was larger than Harvey remembered, about the size of a small barrel. His scales were a dull, lusterless gray, covered in fractal patterns that seemed to absorb what little light there was.

Spitfire laid there like a lump of clay, utterly still. No pulse. No warmth. It looked less like something waiting to jump up into Harvey's arms like it usually did and more like a fossilized geological specimen.

They approached it, their footsteps echoing in the profound silence. Linus scanned it with a new device he was holding. This device had several crystals, forming a . "Readings are… flat. Basal. It's in a state of suspended animation. Hmm. Appears to be deeper than hibernation. It's waiting for a key of some kind to activate."

Harvey reached out, his heart pounding with a futile hope. He placed his hands on Spitfire's snout. "I'm sorry little guy. I don't know what to do."

Spitfire was cold to the touch. Not the cold of stone, but much folder. He felt like the absolute cold of the void between stars. He closed his eyes, reaching inward to listen for the music, for the connection, for the warmth he'd felt in Spitfire. He found only the silence Turing had left him with. The hollow, post-theft static.

He pushed. He concentrated until his head throbbed and his knees felt weak. He begged, pleading with the empty space inside him.

Nothing.

Spitfire remained a cold, dead weight.

After a long minute, he let his hands fall to his sides, his shoulders slumping in defeat.

Linus let out a long, slow breath. "Well," he said, his voice quiet in the vast, silent chamber. "That's a problem."

Linus had always been optimistic, so Harvey's routine hopelessness felt even darker than usual, knowing he was not the only one to feel it.

9

Sentient, Angry Lint

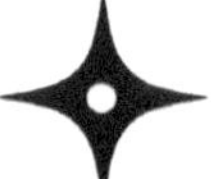

Back in the Grand Crystal Archives, the ruined library felt less like a sanctuary and more like a tomb for bad ideas. Their idea, specifically. Spitfire sat on Linus's obsidian worktable, a gray, fractal paperweight holding down their collective failure. The only sound was the relentless drip-drop-plip-plop from a leak somewhere in the crystal ceiling, a sound that was slowly drilling its way into Harvey's soul.

"It's a joke," Harvey said, his voice flat. He poked the egg with a finger. It felt like poking a glacier. "A cosmic joke. The universe's way of saying 'nice try, now please die quietly.'"

Linus was not listening. "Eh, it does that sometimes. But again, things are not always what they seem." He had dismantled his smartphone-thaumometer hybrid and was now soldering a new component onto the board. "It's not a joke. I think we should view this as an open mic ceremony. There's room for creative interpretation here. There's a difference. A joke implies it was never viable. The open mic implies it's like a crowd waiting for the correct stimulus– the punch line."

"The correct stimulus being a fully-powered dragonbinder, which I am no longer."

"Well, you were never a fully-powered dragonbinder. Remember that was Plan A. I think it's safe to say we are no longer on Plan A or B, but more likely on Plan Q, subsection C," Linus muttered, holding a fancy golden pair of cat eye glasses over a tiny, glowing capacitor. "This plan is, essentially, to try everything until something works or we accidentally open a portal to a dimension of sentient, angry lint."

"Is there a dimension like that?" Harvey was excited to think of all the possibilities.

"There are an infinite number of realities, all living on top of one another at the same time. And yes, Lintoria is real. Let's just say if you are someone that has ever used a vacuum cleaner, you do not want to stumble into Lintoria for any reason."

The idea of such a place existing made Harvey chuckle.

Kael thoughtfully put her hand on her chin. "I only know of two worlds. Aetherium and Earth. And I've never been to Earth before, but obviously I know it exists."

"Ha!" Linus licked the frame of a new pair of glasses he pulled out of his coat pocket. This pair was made of shining mint candy. "Oh, I assure you it's a real place. It's a bit crowded. I don't recommend it. Where did you think all the missing socks go? See, most people think lint forms on socks over time, but actually they Lintorians eat socks. That is why every time you do a load of laundry, at least one sock mysteriously disappears. I hear socks are very high in fiber though."

"I have no need for socks. Socks just slow you down." Kael said, her voice swelling with pride..

Harvey didn't know what he believed anymore. He slumped onto the stool. For days, his internal world had been a flat line. The comfort of his imaginary pet dragon Spitfire, the psychic pressure of Eranthus's call, even the subtle, grumpy pulse of the moss named Steve on his apartment wall—all of it was gone, replaced by a sterile, post-surgical quiet. He was a radio tuned to a dead frequency.

But as he stared at Spitfire's fractal patterns, a memory surfaced. Not a sound, but a feeling. The feeling of his hands on Spitfire's warm scales. The simple, uncomplicated joy of that connection. It wasn't about power. It was about… attention. It was about focusing on something else so completely that you forgot the static in your own head.

He did have a friend, all along. Spitfire was his best friend.

"What if it's not about power?" Harvey said, more to himself than to Linus.

"Oh, everything is about power," Linus replied without looking up. "Thermodynamics, economics, who gets the last slice of deep dish pizza—it's all a power struggle."

"No, I mean… the dragonbinding. You said it yourself. Sometimes things are not what they seem. So, what if it's not about control. It's about resonance. Harmony." He stood up and walked to the table. "What if I'm trying to shout at it, when I should be… listening?"

Linus paused his soldering. "That is both profoundly wise and utterly useless. How, precisely, does one 'listen' to a fossilized dragon toy?"

Harvey didn't answer. He placed both hands on the cold, gray scaly body. He closed his eyes. He didn't try to push. He didn't try to find the missing music. Instead, he focused on the memory of the music. The warmth of Spitfire. The majestic, terrifying beauty of Eranthus's voice screaming *"Dragonbinder!"*

He focused on the feeling of connection, not the fact of its loss. He poured every ounce of that remembered feeling, that nostalgic yearning, into the void where his power used to be. It was a scream into a void, but a scream of longing, not of command.

He felt nothing. Just the same, profound cold.

And then, a flicker.

It was so faint he almost dismissed it as a muscle twitch. A tiny, almost imperceptible pulse of warmth beneath his palms. He gasped, his eyes flying open.

"What?" Linus demanded, setting his tools down. "What is it? Did you short-circuit something?"

"I… I felt something."

Spitfire's scaly skin under his hands began to glow with a deep, rich, molten gold hue. A hairline crack appeared with a sound like a frozen lake breaking in spring.

"By the forgotten hot dog gods of Chicago," Linus whispered, scrambling for his measuring device. "You did it! You surely are the dragonbinder! Whew, what a relief. Okay, you've got it from here then. Save the world and such, I'm off for tea time."

Harvey welcomed the sarcastic humor Linus was giving, it helped lessen the tension he was feeling. Harvey didn't move for a while. He kept his hands on Spitfire, pouring every memory of warmth, every shred of his longing for connection into that single, glowing point. More cracks spider-webbed outwards. The glow intensified, spilling from the fractures and painting the surrounding crystal shelves in hues of amber and honey.

With an abrupt, soft plopping sound, Spitfire's jaw opened. His tiny, wet, scaled head poked up, and he looked up at Harvey like a curious dog. His head was crowned with nubby horns, and its eyes were two pools of reptilian hazel. Spitfire blinked, letting out a squeak that was less a roar and more the sound a rusty hinge would make if it were trying to ask a question.

It looked at Harvey. It sniffed the air, then butted its head against his hand, a clear, instinctual gesture. A bond, instantaneous and pure, snapped into place. It wasn't the roaring symphony of Eranthus, or the comfortable hum of Spitfire. It was a new song. A single, clear, perfect note of belonging.

Harvey laughed, a sound of pure, unadulterated joy he hadn't made since he was a child. He carefully helped the little creature to stand upright. Spitfire was always clumsy, all wings and tail, and it immediately tried to climb up his arm, its tiny claws pricking through his shirt.

"It worked," Harvey breathed, tears stinging his eyes. "Linus, it actually worked."

Linus was frantically taking readings, his device whirring and clicking. He was suddenly wearing dark sunshades, and Harvey had no idea where they came from, and did not see Linus put them on. "A fascinating new development. The thaumic signature between the two of you is... nascent, but pure. Untainted by external code. And it's syncing to your residual frequency. It's like a... a dedicated personal area network of one."

"I didn't realize how much I cared about him until he was gone." Harvey said, patting his friend. The dragonet chirruped in agreement, a small puff of warm, cinnamon-scented smoke erupting curls out of its nostrils.

For the next several hours, they forgot about the stolen power, about the dying dragon. They were just a man, a scholar, a warrior and a newborn dragonet. Linus found a stash of dried, glowing berries that Spitfire devoured with comical enthusiasm. Harvey felt a piece of himself he thought was dead slowly knitting back together around that single, clear note of connection. He didn't have to be the dragonbinder, or anything special at all. He was just a guy with a baby dragon. And that was enough. It was everything.

● ▬▬▬▬▬▬ ● ▬▬▬▬▬▬ ● ▬▬▬▬▬▬ ●

Across the city, in a sub-basement that didn't exist on any architectural blueprint in any known realm, a bank of servers hummed. The room was cold, clean, and lit by the cool blue glow of liquid-cooled processing units. In the center of the room, suspended in a harness of glowing energy, was the skeletal frame of the Aetherblade. It was all sharp angles and polished steel, a dragon-shaped void waiting to be filled.

Alex Turing stood before a large, holographic display. It was a map of the city, overlaid with a shimmering grid of energy signatures. Most were faint, background static. One signal had recently appeared, a steady, pulsing red dot.

It was weak at first, a flicker of gold light on the map, located in the sector corresponding to the old library. But as Turing watched, it intensified, burning brighter and brighter. It wasn't a chaotic, messy signature. It was something purer, simpler. A foundational frequency. A key, turning in a lock.

A slow, genuine smile spread across Turing's face. It was not a pleasant expression.

On his workbench, a small, copper-mesh glove began to glow, resonating with the distant signal. He picked it up, feeling the harmonic vibration in his bones. His calculations were correct, Harvey was indeed the dragonbinder.

He would use Harvey as an energy source, draining him of the dragonbinder power if he needed more. And he would need more. Much more.

Turing knew that he was the only one that could truly handle the power that came with being a dragonbinder. Because he knew something Harvey couldn't possibly know. He knew that evil served as much of a purpose as good, that power was something to be wielded ruthlessly, not stumbled onto like a plaything.

Turing assured himself that he was not evil, everyone else was just an idiot.

"I knew you were the one, Harvey," he whispered to the empty room.

On the holographic display, a targeting reticle, sleek and precise, silently locked onto the blazing golden signal emanating from the Grand Crystal Archives.

10

The Half-life of Joy

Joy had a half-life, and it was far too short. Happiness was a brilliant, unstable element that decayed rapidly into simpler, more stable emotions like anxiety and the nagging suspicion that you've left the oven on. For a short while, the good feelings had been a physical warmth in his chest, a counterpoint to the tiny, sleeping weight of Spitfire curled in the hollow of Harvey's collarbone. The dragon purred when it breathed, a sound like a tiny, contented Geiger counter.

Linus had, for once, stopped tinkering. He was observing a half-eaten bag of barbecue potato chips open on the desk beside a thirteenth-century treatise on ontological paradoxes.

"Fascinating," Linus murmured, not taking his eyes off Spitfire. "The bonding process appears to be creating a localized stabilization field. The dimensional flicker around you has decreased by eighteen percent. It's as if the little beast is a living anchor."

"Thank you for helping me get him back, Linus," Harvey said, a protective edge to his voice. He ran a finger over the dragon's warm, obsidian scales.

"Ah, happy for you and Spitfire. A sentimentally appropriate, if aerodynamically optimistic relationship, if ever there was one." Linus pulled a bag of snacks out of his pocket and crunched another handful of barbecue potato chips cheerfully. *Nomf nomph neruuuumph.* The chips crunched joyfully as they were devoured. "He's currently generating about as much heat as a common pocket warmer. A very expensive, magical, and emotionally needy pocket warmer."

"Aww, I don't think he's needy."

"Anyways, happy to help. That's what family is for."

"Family? I thought we were just friends?" Harvey was puzzled by his friend's pondering.

Linus smiled and looked into Harvey's eyes. "Family is more than the people you are born to, you know. Sometimes it's the people you meet along the way. And family means everything! Yes, you are like a dear brother to me already."

Linus wiped the salt and flavorings from the chips onto his pants, leaving an obvious powdered stain on his impeccably fancy suit, looking needlessly chaotic. His fingers suddenly froze at a shattering, scraping sound.

But it was not just a sound, but rather a thunderous feeling. It was a pressure change, a sudden, painful pop in the eardrums. The floating globes of light in the Archives flickered, their gentle yellow dimming to a sickly orange. The low, comforting hum of the place stuttered, replaced by a high-pitched, teeth-rattling whine.

Spitfire jolted awake, letting out a sharp, frightened cheep. *"Cheep cheep! Cheeeeeep!"* He scrambled, digging his tiny claws into Harvey's shoulder.

"What was that sound?" Harvey asked, his heart starting to hammer.

Linus was already on his feet, his device in his hand, its readings going haywire. "That was–," he said, his voice grim, "I don't know."

The second sound was unmistakable. It was the screech of tearing metal and shattering crystal from the upper levels, racing towards them. It was followed by the rhythmic, pounding thud of heavy, precise footfalls. Not the skittering of the six-legged hounds. This was something new. Something bigger.

"They must be coming this way," Linus said, grabbing a heavy, crystal-and-bronze spyglass from a rack of similar artifacts. He tossed it to Harvey. It was surprisingly heavy. "Here. Use the focusing lens. Point the business end at anything that doesn't look like us and think very rude thoughts. It might give it a slight headache."

Kael breathed a sigh of dismay. "Ugh. You aren't going to do anything with that, stop being silly. She handed her trusty crossbow to Harvey. It was surprisingly heavy. Harvey had never used any type of weapon before, and surely felt uncomfortable with this thing suddenly in his hands.

She pulled a large dagger from a side pocket and wielded it instinctively, in a defensive posture.

"Linus, what is going on? What's coming this way?"

"Plan Q.2 has unforeseen consequences!" Linus shouted over the rising din of destruction from above. "The bond between you and Spitfire perhaps? Maybe it's acting as some kind of a beacon? I'm an idiot! I should have shielded it, dampened it—"

A section of the crystalline ceiling fifty feet away exploded inwards. Through the hole descended a nightmare.

They were humanoid, seven feet tall, with brushed-steel carapaces and featureless silver face plates. In perfect, terrifying unison, they landed on the bejeweled floor, their weight cracking the ancient mosaic. They carried no visible weapons; their hands ended in wicked, scalpel-like probes that hummed with sterile white energy. They were silent. The only sound was the hum of their internal systems and the crunch of broken crystal under their feet.

"These appear to be some kind of sentinel units," Linus breathed.

One of the sentinels' head-plates swiveled. Its blank face fixed on Harvey— or more precisely, on the shivering, glowing form of Spitfire on his shoulder. It raised a hand, and the probe began to glow brighter. They were coming for Spitfire.

Harvey, acting on an instinct he didn't know he had, fired a bolt out of the crossbow, nearly missing one of the sentinels, but scraping its side.

They were a mix of flesh and wire, some kind of hideous cyborg. Wires dangled out where the bolt had nicked the flesh.

Harvey took a deep, short breath and pulled back the lever to reload the crossbow. He aimed better this time and fired a bolt tinged with his own panic, striking the Sentinel square in the chest. The abomination staggered back, a blackened scorch mark on its chassis, but it did not fall. Its head tilted, as if recalculating.

"Good job, Harvey!" Linus yelled, fumbling with something on his workbench. "The crossbow is clearly more effective than a spyglass and negative thoughts. Now do that about twenty more times!"

More dragonets dropped through the hole, their landing forming a perfect, encroaching circle. Harvey backed away, clutching the crossbow, Spitfire clinging to his neck and keening with fear. He fired again, and again. Each bolt slowed them, but they adapted, their carapaces shimmering to disperse the energy. They were adapting, and preparing for his next move.

"We need to get to the portal!" Harvey shouted.

"The portal is likely compromised!" Linus countered. He had pulled a large, jury-rigged device from under the table—two car batteries connected by a nest of wires to a large, cloudy quartz crystal.

Harvey nervously looked at Linus. "Likely? Likely? How likely is it that we can make it out of here? Now isn't the time for calculations, Linus."

"We need a new exit! I just need ninety seconds!"

He never got them.

With a sound like the sky tearing in half, the entire central dome of the Archives was ripped away. Hovering there, blotting out the swirling colors of the Aetherium sky, was the Aetherblade.

It was a gargantuan-sized perversion of a dragon. A skeleton of polished chromium, larger than a commercial airliner, with vast, metallic wings that beat the air with a deafening, hydraulic whine. Where its heart should have been was a pulsating core of captured white energy, and in its empty eye sockets burned twin searchlights that swept across the ruined library. It looked like death itself, rendered anatomically logical and efficient.

The monster's glaring yellow eyes shot out searchlights that locked onto Harvey. Harvey felt a surge of fear as the dragon's glowing eyes pierced his soul. This creature was unreal.

A bay door hissed open on the Aetherblade's undercarriage. A different kind of dragonet emerged, rappelling down on makeshift cables. These dragonets were smaller, faster, and they moved with a single-minded purpose straight for him.

Linus saw it. His gaze went back and forth from the oncoming dragonets to his unfinished escape device, to Harvey's terrified face. He sighed, a sound of profound, academic annoyance.

"Oh, for the love of knowledge," he muttered. "If we make it out of this one I may take up drinking."

The device slipped from his hands and crashed to the floor, wires snapping. Then he did something inexplicable. He grabbed a heavy, leather-bound grimoire from a nearby desk and ran—not away, but directly towards the advancing line of Sentinels.

"Hey!" he shouted, his voice cracking. "You over-engineered, cold-blooded beasts! Read a book!"

He swung the book. It was a pathetically futile gesture. The lead dragonet didn't even break stride. It backhanded him with a force that sent Linus flying across the slippery marble floor. He hit a bookshelf made of living crystal with a sickening crunch of bone and a shower of splintered quartz.

"LINUS!" Harvey screamed.

He tried to run to him, but a dragonet blocked his path. He could only watch as Linus dragged himself up against the shattered shelf, his glasses askew, one lens cracked. He was smiling that thin, brittle smile, a trickle of blood tracing a line from his lip.

"It's okay dear friend," Linus coughed, a wet, horrible sound. "Remember, things aren't always what they seem."

The Aetherblade above them pulsed. A wave of invisible energy slammed down, a null-field designed not to destroy, but to sever. It passed through Harvey like an ice-water enema.

The effect on Spitfire was immediate and horrific. The dragonet screamed, a shrill, psychic shriek of pain and confusion. The warm, golden bond in Harvey's mind—the single, clear note he had fought so hard to find—was snipped cleanly, like a wire. One moment, Spitfire was a part of him. The next moment, he was just a terrified animal.

The little dragon, disoriented and alone, flapped off Harvey's shoulder, directly into the path of a descending dragonet. A delicate, net-like field of energy shot from the construct's hand, enveloping Spitfire. There was a final, desperate chirp, and then the net constricted, and the dragonet was gone, hauled up into the belly of the Aetherblade.

Harvey stood paralyzed, the crystal rod falling from his numb fingers. The warmth in his chest was gone. The silence was back, deeper and more absolute than ever.

The dragonets, their primary objective achieved, began their retreat, ascending on their cables of light. They had came for Spitfire, and they got him. The Aetherblade, with a final, contemptuous beat of its metal wings, turned and vanished into the bruised sky.

The short brutal war was over. It lasted less than three minutes.

Harvey stumbled through the wreckage, over to the broken bookshelf. He slid to his knees beside Linus. His friend's breathing was shallow, each inhalation a ragged, bubbling struggle.

Harvey knew it must be bad. He had heard the sound of something breaking when Linus had been attacked.

"You will be okay." Harvey wasn't sure if he was telling Linus, or just trying to comfort himself at this point.

Linus looked Harvey in the eyes. There wasn't fear in them. He looked joyful. "I enjoyed meeting you, Harvey." Linus managed, his cracked glasses reflecting the fading light. He glanced over to the book he had used as a weapon. "Is the book okay?"

His hand, smeared with blood and dust, twitched, and then was still. The intellectual light behind his eyes winked out.

Harvey knelt there, in the ruins of a library between worlds, the body of his first true friend growing cold beside him. He was suddenly all alone. No Spitfire. No Linus. The prophecy was just the punchline to a sick, twisted joke apparently.

What was the point of any of this?

The dragonbinder was just the same as he had been before any of this started. A broken boy in a broken room, with nothing left to bind, and a silence so profound he was afraid it would swallow him whole.

III

Part Three

Dragons, and Robots, and Spaceships, Oh My!

11

The Technocrat

Few Years ago:

Dr. Alex Turing sat fidgeting, unable to sleep. He scrolled on social media, searching for any kind of distraction he could find. A meme, a viral sports challenge, a clip of a new, edgy comedian. Anything to get his mind off of the news he'd just received of an unfavorable diagnosis for his daughter Lily's health. She was four years old.

Only four.

And the chemo was no longer working.

Lily had already been through so much. Her mother had died less than a year ago. And now this? It felt like it was just too much. He had searched for answers in all the channels he could think of. He tried religion, he tried science, he tried looking into alternative technologies. Nothing held any promise for improving his daughter's outcome.

He hadn't even told her about her illness, he didn't think she was ready to handle that news, and what four year old would be ready for that kind of thing anyways?

His faith had been shaken at the loss of his wife, and now it felt like it was just gone. How could he believe in anything, when all around all he saw was chaos? If he could change anything to make life better, he would. But that didn't matter, because he wasn't the one in charge. He wasn't the one funding cancer research. He wasn't the one shutting funding down either. He just felt, helpless…

The most recent appointment really hit him with some bad news. Lily was possibly looking at her last few months. The doctors could not find any treatment that was working to cure or even treat what was happening to her.

Turing felt like he might cry, weep even. Except he had no more tears. Those tears had poured after losing his wife. And they came steadily after the news of his daughter's illness. But now, the skin beneath his eyes was dry and inflamed, and no tears fell. His pupils grew large with despair.

Turing decided to devote his time, all his time, to his scientific work. If there were no answers to be found in this world, he would simply need to look in another.

His research into quantum mechanics had led him to discover that there were indeed parallel universes that existed, essentially on top of our own. And he began to develop ways to communicate with those realms. He met a being that called himself Azyr, who helped him to figure out the mechanics of inter dimensional travel. Soon he found himself exploring the land of Aetherium. That would be a tale for another book entirely. Or perhaps a small library of many books. But alas, this is not that book.

Turing found that time flowed differently in the Aetherium. It flowed much, much more slowly. Not only did aging seem to slow down there, it seemed to actually reverse. He decided he could take his daughter with him. He felt he was on to something, with this new treatment plan he was devising.

The Aetherium was a marvelous, beautiful place and all, but it just didn't have the same opportunities for Lily. Turing wanted her to experience life the way her mother would have wanted. He wanted her to grow old and go to college, maybe someday start a family of her own.

Due to the fluctuation of time in the Aetherium, he and Lily spent much time together. What felt like years flew by, and she was so happy there. But Turing became full of regret and jealousy of their previous lives. Why should they have to escape to live here? She deserved to live a happy life and be with her friends. Have all the same experiences he had growing up. Why should she be robbed of that? Her first love, finding her career, growing up with dreams of her own. These are the things he wanted for her, more than anything.

The land of Aetherium was full of knowledge, there were more books here than in reality. More books, more knowledge, more– power... He stumbled onto many different types of studies.

He also noted that the Aetherium had changed his daughter. She was slowly changing, into a child much more spoiled, much more entitled. She began making demands about what he should do with his time.

The Aetherium also changed Turing. His desire for things to be his way turned into an unfathomable need. It was no longer just a matter of wanting things to be different, he would force his will upon reality at any cost. Turning could see the change in his daughter, but was oblivious to his own nature changing.

His studies led him down a road of curiosity. This land had science, magic and will. If only he could find a way to bring these energies to the real world.

Then one day he found it. In Codex Dragonis IV, he discovered the source of power. Dragons. The heart of these beings was a source of unfathomable power, able to shift reality (and other realities), to the dragon's will. He only needed to learn how to harness that power. He then stumbled on the stories of the dragonbinder.

He was back in the real world now. The stories of him and his daughter in the Aetherium could fill multiple volumes of books on their own. But the place had changed her, and not for the better. His sweet daughter was no longer there, she had become drunk with power, much like him.

Now that he had his artificial dragon created, he could manipulate the matter in the real world to his will. He could cure his daughter and they could live the life he always wanted.

He thought of his student Harvey, briefly. A part of him wondered if he was wrong to just steal the power from him, perhaps he could have convinced him to help. But the risk was simply too great. He couldn't risk the answer being no. And it was just a student, after all. Not a brilliant, accomplished doctor like him. Surely he knew what was best, not the boy.

There's no way Harvey would help him after he had just failed him. So his power needed to be stolen, and there was no way around it.

His plan was in motion, and he planned an event to turn on the Quantum Siphonator. He would use the device to transfer the power of the dragon from one realm to the next. It worked much like gene editing, but on a much more meta scale. He would use the code found in the other reality to make the real world better. He could already hear the sound of raving crowds, bellowing to his wisdom. They would cheer and clap for his discovery, and the rafters would shake with joyous proclamation.

He would win many awards, and be adored for generations. He heard their roaring praise. To him, it sounded like static.

12

The Absence of Sound

The silence after the attack in the Crystal Archives had a physical weight, a thick, suffocating dust made of pulverized crystal and extinct hopes. Harvey sat on the floor, his back against the shattered obsidian worktable, Linus's body a still, dark shape a few feet away. He didn't cry. The part of him that could produce tears felt as dead and scorched as the dragonet he'd blasted. He was just… empty. He had once been a vessel that had been filled with strange, terribly beautiful music, and was now not only empty, but cracked. A shattered jar of clay.

The Aetherblade was gone, thankfully. But Spitfire and Linus were also gone. The warmth was gone. The void in his head was no longer just the absence of sound; it was a positive force, a cold, sucking vacuum. He was a radio that hadn't just lost its signal, but had its internal wiring ripped out.

He didn't know how long he sat there. Time had become a theoretical concept, like justice or Leo being able to assemble a piece of furniture. The floating light-globes had mostly died, leaving the vast chamber in a deep, bruised twilight. The only illumination came from a few stubborn patches of glowing moss on the far walls and the faint, dying flicker from the wreckage of Linus's escape device.

He suddenly heard the voice of Eranthus in his mind. *"Calm your heart, dear boy."*

"I can't. I just don't see the point of going on anymore. The world is too dark, the times are too trying. I've lost too much to go on."

"Oh, Harveyyyyyyyyyyyyyy." Eranthus voice was deep and comforting. "I know the reason you should go on. You are the reason. You and people like you. People willing to ask why, you are the reason why. You see, so many people never ask that question. They have their reasons already. Power, money, beauty, they are blinded by their lusts. But you, you are none of these things, you want none of these things. You are good, Harvey. That is why you are chosen to be the dragonbinder. The power chose you, because you never would have sought it for yourself."

Harvey felt unsure if what Eranthus was saying was true, but the words brought him great comfort. "I am sorry they made me take Spitfire. I'm being controlled against my will, you must know that. They are using these technologies to control my every move. Yet, there is a part of me deep in my soul they cannot erase. That is what is speaking to you now."

It suddenly dawned on Harvey, Eranthus was the Aetherblade! The giant horrible creature they had encountered was none other than Eranthus himself. He had been corrupted beyond recognition. "It was you? Oh no, what has he done to you..."

Eranthus paused, then continued. "Do not worry about me, boy. I used the last of my strength to send you this message. I don't know if I will be able to speak to you again. My body is just a shell now, I am no longer there. I believe in you Harvey. That is why I summoned you here, to the Aetherium."

"What do I do now?" Harvey asked. He waited, and waited more. There was no reply. Eranthus was gone, that was all that had remained of his strength.

For all he knew, this was all just a dream. His newfound friends, the dragon yelling into his mind, it was all just nonsense. It couldn't be real. But the grief felt real. Losing Linus felt real.

Harvey's gaze drifted, unfocused, over the carnage. Scorched spots on the star-chart floor from his own panicked blasts. A single, cracked lens from

Linus's spectacles glinting in the low light. A scattered pile of papers that had been swept off the desk in the struggle.

One of the papers had drifted to rest against his foot. It was covered in Linus's cramped, precise handwriting, a mix of complex formulae and exasperated marginalia. Harvey stared at it, not really seeing it. The words were just shapes. Then, a phrase, heavily circled and underlined, snagged on the broken edge of his consciousness.

"...rejects standard thaumic induction. Hypothesis: touching the sword of remembrance cou–..."

He couldn't make out the rest of that note. Harvey's breath hitched. He picked up the paper, his fingers trembling. He scanned the other scattered pages, scooping them up, his movements becoming frantic. He wasn't looking for a grand plan or a secret weapon. He was looking for a ghost. For the sound of his friend's voice.

He found more notes, scribbled on the backs of takeout menus, in the margins of textbooks, on a napkin that smelled vaguely of barbecue sauce. Linus sure did enjoy barbecue, which was surprising how thin he was.

A scrumped, faded yellow note read:

Dragonbinder Theory 218: Subject C.H. exhibits zero control aptitude, yet spontaneous resonance events occur in proximity to non-threatening entities (see: moss cluster "Steve," draconian familiar "Spitfire"). Contradiction? Or a different paradigm? Focused will?

Harvey began digging a grave for Linus.

He didn't know the rites of the Aetherium, and the idea of dragging his friend's body through a dimensional portal to a city morgue felt wrong. So, in a quiet corner of the ruined Archives where the floor was no longer intact and had given way to exposed dirt, he used a piece of shattered crystal to dig. It was slow, brutal work. The ground beneath the mosaic was a compacted, clay-like substance. He was determined to give his friend a proper burial, but after a few minutes his arms were already starting to give out.

He dug for hours, until the hurt was more specific. It was no longer just his arms that hurt. His bones hurt. His heart hurt. But feeling something other than the impending loss actually seemed helpful. He found that he didn't mind the physical pain of exertion, it actually brought him comfort, because for those moments he was feeling something else. Anything else.

When the grave was dug, he placed Linus inside, along with his cracked spectacles and the empty bag of barbecue chips. He had nothing to mark the grave but a simple, smooth river stone from the path in the caves. It felt insufficient. It was all he had.

He stood over the patch of disturbed earth for a long time, the new silence in his head no longer empty, but filled with the ghost of a sarcastic, brilliant voice. "Things aren't always what they seem." Harvey truly wished those words were true. Because things sure seemed hopeless.

Kael's voice suddenly appeared, as she walked up to Harvey. "Most people believe the Binder commands the dragon. I don't think that is how it works though. Most displays of power are just loud weakness on display. True power is in silence, in listening. My mother taught me that growing up on our farm in a town not far from here. So I believe the role of the dragonbinder is actually to listen. To hear the dragon, and in doing so, allow the world to listen to hear the dragon's song too. So the dragonbinder is more of a translator than a general. But that's just my opinion. I've never met a dragonbinder before."

"Your mother told you stories about dragons on a farm? That's so wild, where I'm from farms are for cheese and that's about it." Harvey cracked a faint smile, thinking of the land he was from. "I don't suppose she told you any story about a sword of remembrance? I saw that on one of Linus' notes."

"As a matter of fact, she did." Kael looked down, a sense of sorrow coming over her as well. "She told us many stories, that is what our people did. It's the way the elders would pass on what they knew to younger generations. And they would record their stories into these crystals. Anyways, the sword of remembrance is a real legendary artifact actually, but I've never seen it. It belongs to The Nexus Prince. Anyone can use that sword to remember their power, but The Nexus Prince is who it belongs to, because he has the power over all realms. I think it may give him special abilities too, but who knows. We haven't had a Nexus Prince in a very long time. He disappeared and no one knows where he went. My mother was a firm believer, but it's been so long without one, I think it was just a myth."

"That's insane. I was totally kidding about a sword of remembrance. That's quite hilarious such a thing would exist. One more question though—What makes The Nexus Prince special?" Harvey kicked a rock.

"What makes anyone special?" Kael countered.

"Eh. I don't know."

Harvey's heart began to pound, a dull, painful thud in the silence. The ghost of Linus echoed in his mind. Not Linus in his final, heroic moment, but in the quiet, messy moments before. The way he'd measured the thaumic field without judgment. The way he'd called Spitfire an "emotionally needy pocket warmer" while carefully noting its preferred brand of lichen. He was special.

He thought of Spitfire, the simple, uncomplicated trust of a creature that saw his "unstable psyche" as a perfectly normal home. He hadn't commanded it. He'd just… paid attention. He'd fed it. He'd given it a name.

His friendship with Spitfire had been forged in a moment of shared vulnerability, of him pouring his own loneliness and longing into the void of the universe.

The epiphany didn't arrive with a clap of thunder or a burst of light. It was quieter, sadder, and far more profound. It settled over him like a shroud, but a shroud that was also a map.

Perhaps Kael was right. His power as a dragonbinder had never been about his own strength. How could it be? He was Harvey Chandler, a failed architecture student with a prescription for anti-psychotics and a roommate who argued with furniture. He was a collection of inadequacies held together by anxiety and cheap coffee. (He had a penchant for a certain orange-labeled brand that paired well with donuts, but whatever was on clearance usually won.)

His power was about connection. It was about perception. He wasn't the lead singer in the cosmic band; he was the conductor. His role wasn't to sing the loudest, but to hear every other voice—the brave, cynical melody of Linus, the fierce, protective rhythm of Kael, the simple, warm harmony of Spitfire, the pure, new note of Spitfire—and help them find their key. To bind them together into something greater than the sum of their parts.

The dragonbinder didn't bind dragons. He bound himself. He bound all his fears, and his hopes alike. That must be how it worked. It was never about power, it was about something more zen. He was a channel, a conduit of energy.

He looked at Linus's still form, and the grief was suddenly a sharp, clean pain, not a numb void. Linus hadn't died for a prophecy. He'd died for a friend. He'd died protecting a connection. It was the most powerful, illogical, human magic there was. Here in this magical realm, this place of impossibilities, he had seen a magical being do the most human act of selflessness. That was the power of a true leader. Not in holding the power in themselves, but being able to see it in others. To help everyone else to grow into their own power. Yes, that had to be it!

Slowly, Harvey got to his feet. The silence was still there, but it was different now. It was no longer an emptiness to be feared. It was the space between notes, necessary for the music to exist. It was a listening silence.

He imagined this must be how a musician feels when they finally write a song after a long dry spell. Or when they pick up an instrument after years of collecting dust, just so they can go through the motions of day to day life.

"How would we locate the sword of remembrance?" Harvey asked.

"Well, again I've never seen it. But I believe it is somewhere nobody would ever find it. It's in your world."

"Really? Where?"

"The museum in your city. Even for museums, it's a rarely visited place. The elders thought it would be the most effective place to hide it, a place nobody would ever look. The place where it would make sense to put a sword. In a museum."

Harvey thought back over his life, and sure enough he couldn't recall much of the museum. He had been there for sure, but it was so small he couldn't identify anything of interest from his visit there.

"If you want to go there to look for it, put your hand here on this device and think peaceful thoughts. It will center your resonance back to your home."

"Do you do everything with crystals?" Harvey asked, half-joking, but also totally serious.

Kael looked over to him with a sly grin. "Yeah, now that you mention it. I guess we do."

Harvey didn't know how to solder wires or re-calibrate energy fields. But he knew the warmth of Spitfire. He thought of the sharp, intellectual spark of Linus's mind. He acquiesced the fierce, protective heat of Kael's spirit. He held those feelings in his heart, not as a command, but as an invitation. He had friends now, in this place. He had peaceful thoughts.

He placed his hand on the jagged edge of the cold quartz crystal.

He didn't push. He didn't demand it. He simply focused and listened into the silence, waiting for an answer.

Deep within the dead crystal, a single, microscopic point of light winked into existence. It was fainter than a forgotten star, weaker than the last ember in a cold fireplace.

But it was there.

13

Memes of a Dog in a Raincoat, etc.

Harvey suddenly found himself opening the jingling door of the city museum. The exhibits were silent, as the museum appeared to be empty. Harvey glanced at a clock and saw it was three pm, likely open. This made it even more shocking it was so empty. His hands were near his mouth and he was eating something that he didn't remember deciding to eat. He pulled it out of his mouth and his eyes widened in disappointment and disgust. It was a gnarly patch of the same blue-green moss that he had loved to find names for. He truly hoped this wasn't the one he had dubiously dubbed Leonard, when they had arrived at the library earlier. And it absolutely better not be Steve! Somehow, it seemed that was the logical conclusion, if there was such a thing anymore.

"There it is." Kael pointed straight ahead to a sword on display on top of a counter. It didn't look like it was secured at all, and there was no staff nearby.

Harvey wondered why this sword of memory would be left alone if it had such value. Perhaps the curators of the museum weren't aware of its power, that must be the explanation.

The sword had a beckoning aura, a hum that seemed to get stronger and louder as Harvey approached. "That's odd, I can hear the sword."

"That's how it works. It will tell you who you are. Go and touch it." Kael beckoned him to continue.

Harvey touched the blade, and it felt just like any other cold steel. But then a whirring pulse that seemed to shine through Harvey's mind. "I–I–I remember now. I am the dragonbinder."

Kael smiled at him. "I knew it. So, now what?"

They noticed there was an old woman who was sleeping behind the counter. The world outside was the same: gray, drizzling, and relentlessly normal. For the first time, he was grateful for it. He was grateful just to be dull Harvey, in a dreary, boring world again.

"I'm not sure exactly. I kind of wish we could just stay here a while. Maybe I could show you some video games or something."

"Harvey, we kind of need to save all of reality first. Then, yes you can show me your games." Kael chuckled, nervously. Did people of Harvey's age still play games as adults?

Harvey saw something else on the counter. It was that book again… The paperback book titled "The Nexus Prince." It must have been a tale from many years ago, as evidenced from the half-torn sale sticker on its spine from a successful small-town garage sale. He must have picked it up and read it at some point.

THE NEXUS
PRINCE

Harvey couldn't say when the last time he read anything other than a textbook was. He picked up the book and fingered to a random page. It read:

True power is no power at all. And there is no power that can be taken, only given.

Harvey sighed. "I'm even more confused than before. What is that supposed to mean?"

"No clue. You're the dragonbinder."

Harvey and Kael stepped outside of the library, and saw that the sky was beginning to darken. It was right before dusk, where the sun kisses the earth and produces a dazzling display of colors before cuddling itself into darkness.

The color that lit up the sky above them was a brilliant dark indigo that danced in the reflection of Harvey's eyes. Kael saw the glimmer in his eyes, and for the first time felt a sense of compassion towards the outsider. He was a good man, a soft caring man. She began to understand the concept of grief, and wondered if she had felt it in her world as well. Her training had led her to abandon all feelings, they were nothing but a burden for a warrior such as her. But maybe her training had been wrong. Maybe the feelings made her a better warrior.

His apartment was a time capsule of his own collapse. The Björkön bookshelf was now perched at a solid forty-five-degree angle, held in place by a complex system of shoelaces and what looked like Leo's entire collection of graphic novels. The crooked floor had caused Leo to improvise a solution to make it steady and square. Leo himself was on the couch, staring at the tower of particle board with the hollow-eyed stare of a man who had seen the face of true chaos.

"I think it's mocking me," Leo said, not looking up as Harvey entered. "I swear I heard it sigh when I walked past. It's a monument to my failure as a man."

Harvey and Kael stood in the doorway, rainwater dripping from their hair.

He looked at his roommate, really looked at him. Not as an obstacle to his secret life, or a representative of the mundane world he was trying to escape, but as Leo. The guy who made terrible coffee and brilliant observations, who fought with furniture and never once asked Harvey why he sometimes stared at walls for hours and talked to imaginary friend dragon plushies.

"Leo, meet Kael". Harvey said, his voice rough from disuse, but somehow gleaming with a newfound confidence.

Leo finally turned. He took in Harvey's soaked clothes, the dirt under his fingernails, the new, grim set to his jaw. And–a woman. "Umm—hi." He stood up urgently and walked over to shake her hand. "I'm Leo, nice to—meet you."

"Leo, let's go out for some sushi? I've got a hankering for some wasabi, and sushi always helps me think creatively."

"Okay, I'm all ears. I don't know if we can afford sushi though, man. Did you finally get a job? Please tell me you got a job. We're down to the cheapest kind of ramen they sell. Not only that, we only have chicken flavor left." He glanced over at the kitchen counter, which housed several boxes full of ramen packets. Sometimes stereotypes were a thing because they were based on some semblance of truth. This was one of those cases. College students all eat ramen. Yes, that appeared to be the case.

"No, it's not about a job," Harvey said. He walked over and sat on the arm of the couch, keeping a safe distance from the Björkön's gravitational field. "Well, not a job exactly. But a role, you could say. I also need to tell you about… a different world. A place called the Aetherium. There's a city that exists on top of our own, and you would probably love it there. Lots of bookshelves! Except they house crystals instead of books. And–Spitfire's real, believe it or not."

Leo looked at his roommate in disbelief, glancing across the room at the pill bottle on the counter top. "Your stuffed animal? Harvey–it's just a toy dude. Like for real man, you sound nuts sometimes."

"He's telling you the truth." Kael chimed in.

Leo realized that there was a slight possibility that Harvey might actually be telling the truth. If he wasn't, and this was just some elaborate story, then what could explain him suddenly having a female friend, especially one with such a detailed and realistic looking renaissance fair-esque costume. And what was that…Leo blurted out, "Wait, is that a crossbow?!"

"Sit down, Leo. I will explain everything."

For the next hour, Harvey talked. He told Leo about seeing the moss on the walls, about Spitfire being more than a plush toy, about a friend named Linus who had just died in a library that didn't exist. He told him about a man who was building a mechanical dragon, and a little, stolen dragonet named Spitfire. He kept his voice flat, factual. He was not asking for belief. He was presenting data.

When he finished, the only sound was the drip from the kitchen faucet and the low hum of the refrigerator.

Leo was silent for a long time. He leaned forward, elbows on his knees, and stared at the stained carpet. Then he said, "So that's why you always flinched when a bird flew past the window. It's all starting to make sense now."

Harvey blinked. "What?"

"You thought it was one of the… spectral draconic forms, or whatever. I noticed. I just thought you had a weird thing about pigeons." Leo looked up, and his eyes were clear and focused. "This Linus guy. He was real to you?"

"Yes."

"And he's dead."

"Yes." Harvey looked down, saddened.

Leo nodded slowly. He looked over at the critically listing bookshelf, then back at Harvey. "Okay. So. And your teacher, Professor Turing. He's like the ultimate, evil version of the IKEA instructions, right? Taking something beautiful and complex and trying to turn it into a sterile, logical, soul-crushing piece of crap. Like living, breathing pop radio?"

A surprised, wet sound that was almost a laugh escaped Harvey's throat. "Yeah. That's… that's exactly what he is. He's trying to gain power at the world's expense."

"Right. So we can't have that." Leo stood up, cracking his knuckles. "What's the plan, chief? Do we burn down the metaphorical house?"

"No," Harvey said, a strange, warm feeling spreading through his chest, a feeling that had nothing to do with magic and everything to do with not being alone. "I think he wants a fight. Will you help us?"

Leo agreed to. "You better not be just playing games, or have this be some kind of elaborate prank. But if the fate of the universe is at stake, count me in. If for no other reason, for curiosity's sake. I want to see if this is all real."

Over the next two days, Harvey made a list of people who had almost been his friends. He realized he might need all the help he can get to take on the Aetherblade. It was a short, sad list, composed of people he had systematically pushed away. Brenda, from his gym class, who seemed way out of his league. And Mark, a guy from his one semester in a film elective, who had always invited him to weird indie movie screenings.

He met them separately, in noisy, brightly lit coffee shops that felt aggressively real. He gave them the same speech, the explanation that made no sense to them, but he told it with such truth and passion they were at least willing to entertain him. Brenda, pragmatic and sharp, had asked a series of probing, architectural questions about the structural integrity of the floating citadel. How could such a building exist? It just didn't make sense.

Mark, who saw the world through a lens of cinematic tropes, had simply nodded and said, "So you see things nobody else can see. Like that movie from the '80s with the guy wearing the special sunglasses, but with dragons instead of aliens. Gotcha." His comments were always followed by a doubting glare, even if not being proposed such otherworldly tales.

Somehow Mark was even more of a geek than Harvey, and that is quite a statement. But Harvey realized that he had shut these people out for some invisible reason. They had reached out to him as friends, but he wasn't ready to be himself and have friends yet. He felt ready now.

And he needed friends now. He needed them to send him a text when they saw something beautifully, mundanely real. He needed them to send him food reviews with pictures of a perfectly poured latte. Memes of a dog in a raincoat, etc. To be the chorus that reminded him what this world sounded like, so he could remember the beautiful things of this world sometimes, and drown out the dissonance from the other.

Simultaneously, he walked the thinner places of the Aetherium. He was now able to walk between both realms at will, he didn't have to be stuck in one or the other. He wondered what the catalyst for this development had been. Perhaps it was the grief. It was surely a powerful emotion. It shook him to his very core. Such profound hurt, loss, sorrow, yet he felt a warm glow that persisted.

He didn't go to the powerful Charred Council or seek out great warriors. He went to the edges. He found a grove of the faeries Linus had documented— skittish, jewel-bright creatures that communicated in flickers of light. He didn't try to command them, or convince him to join his battle. He just opened his heart to them, and hoped they would do the same in return. He sat at the edge of their grove for hours, listening to the silent, frantic poetry of their light-show, until one, bolder than the rest, landed on his knee and showed him a memory of the sky before Turing's smog.

"My name is Gleela. Me and my people will help you!" She proclaimed.

He tracked a small flock of star-dragons, cousins to Spitfire, who nested in the magnetic fields around the city's radio towers. He didn't ask them to fight. He asked them to join him. He asked them to sing the song of Eranthus, the true song, before it was corrupted.

He was not building an army. He was building a network of friends and connections, large and small, across two worlds. His new plan was not a weapon to destroy the Aetherblade. It was a key.

Turing's power was a bootleg, a sterile copy of the dragonbinder's power. Harvey's plan was to disrupt that artificial signal by flooding it with the one thing it couldn't replicate: the chaotic, beautiful, innate will of the creatures Turing sought to control. He would amplify the cry of the song of Eranthus until it shattered the machine's silence.

Turing may be mad with intellect in the Aetherium, but on Earth he's still just a man. And men, as mad as they may be, still have a hint of reason buried within. Harvey didn't know if this was really true, but he believed and hoped that it was.

He stood on his apartment's fire escape, looking out at the city lights superimposed over the Glimmering Spires. He held his phone, on which was a picture from Brenda of a pigeon triumphantly standing on a sleeping cat. He felt the memory of the crystalline sprite's trust, a tiny, cool point of light in his mind. He listened for the echo of the star-dragons' memories. Fractured memories would enter his brain of the way Linus made him laugh. He thought of his parents and how he longed to know them, if only he had the chance. And now he feel more of that same longing, but for his friend.

The chorus of this choir was sure to be small and fragile. But for the first time, Harvey was no longer the only one singing. He was listening. He was listening to the song of everything around him, and it was a beautiful composition indeed. He heard a thick brassy hum, singing strings, harmonious harps, electric guitars crunching, saxophones swaying, pianos plucking. It was coming back to him now. He was the dragonbinder.

14

The End of Two Worlds

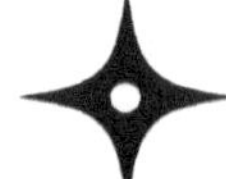

The end of two worlds begins with a car. There were no ominous proclamations, no dramatic declarations of war broadcast on all channels. More specifically, it started with Harvey trying to figure out how to fit everyone into his rusted, textbook-filled Honda Civic.

Harvey looked at the parking ticket sitting on the dash, and hid it under the visor. Hopefully he would pay it later, but he prioritized saving the world as a more important matter at this time. He was a fine driver, but he couldn't ask Kael to drive. Why, you ask? Well, cars didn't exist in the Aetherium.

PARKING VIOLATION
NOTICE
This vehicle is improperly parked
Violations are as follows
Parked in No Parking Area/Space
Parked in Fire Lane
Parked in Handicap Space
Parked in Reserved/Assigned Space
Blocking Driveway or Access
Blocking Other Vehicle
Parked Too Close to Hydrant
Parked in Multiple Spaces
Other
DATE
CENSE P ATE NO
T ME
ISSUED BY
VEH C E MAKE/MODEL
Honda Civic
FINE: $ $

Kael stared the others up and down, and looked to Brenda. "You have the makings of a warrior, but your armor is a kind I have not seen before."

"Um, thanks?" Brenda said, confused. This woman is pretty serious about her cosplay, she thought to herself.

"What are we doing with this device, exactly?" Kael pondered aloud.

"It's a car. It will get us to Turing faster."

Harvey thought to himself: I can drive. Kael in the front seat. Leo, Brenda and Mark in the back seat. This would be a tight fit indeed, as Mark was notably chubbier than his peers.

"What exactly are we going to do again?" Brenda asked. She didn't actually believe anything Harvey had said, but was incredibly bored and felt she could use a break from watching reality television show reruns, so she had decided to tag along.

As the car began to drive, Harvey noticed that Kael seemed to dig her hands into the seat, nervously. It was fascinating to see a hardened warrior like her losing her bearings on her first car ride, but she was not likely to say anything about it.

The car went onto a highway, and Kael took off her boot and projectile vomited into it. She then took the other boot off. "I don't need these anyways" she boasted, wiping the thick, foul-smelling vomit from her chin.

"Oh my God!" Brenda exclaimed. "That's disgusting!"

● ━━━━━━ ● ━━━━━━ ● ━━━━━━ ●

A fleet of ominous black vans, identical and silent, were double-parking directly in front of the university's Turing Center for Particle Physics. They disgorged men and women in crisp, fashionably gray suits who moved with the same unnerving synchronicity as Turing's dragonets, cordoning off the block with a quiet, bureaucratic authority that was more terrifying than any show of force.

"Alright team, everybody spread out and let's see if we can find my dragon. Operation Spitfire is a go." Harvey whispered into the hodgepodge walkie talkie system they had built with a cell phone app and cheap headphones.

From his vantage point in the geology building across the quad, Harvey watched as Turing emerged from his fancy, expensive laboratory with armed guards as he mounted the stage. Harvey saw the real-world vans, but he also saw the Aetherium-layer: the vans were crystalline siege points, and the uniformed personnel were definitely Turing's dragonets, their featureless face plates glinting under the campus's fluorescent streetlights. The two realities were so perfectly aligned here, at this Nexus point, that there was almost no distinction left.

"Showtime," Mark whispered, crouched beside him with a laptop open, its screen a mess of code and a pirated live-feed of the campus security cameras. "The man himself just arrived. The suit is still impeccable. I'd give it a 9.5 for villainous chic, points deducted for lack of a flamboyant cape. I'm gonna record this and go viral to pay for college."

In Harvey's other ear, a cheap Bluetooth headset crackled. "The... uh... 'specimen relocation' is underway," Brenda's voice came through, tight with stress. She was posing as a grad student, her tool belt full of actual wrenches and one of Linus's leftover thaumic disruptors, which looked suspiciously like a garage door opener wrapped in copper wire. "They're wheeling in a big crate on a hydraulic lift."

Harvey imagined if Linus were able to be here he would likely say something along the lines of "That's the kind of crate you use for something that's either a nuclear reactor or a very, very large and angry parrot."

"It must be the Aetherblade's power core is around here somewhere," Harvey said, his voice calm. A strange serenity had settled over him. The frantic fear was gone, replaced by the low, steady hum of the network. He could feel them all, a constellation of consciousness focused on this single, fragile point in spacetime.

He saw Leo, a bright knot of manic energy, who was currently using his hard-won knowledge of structural weakness to "accidentally" reroute a main power conduit through the building's sprinkler system. He felt the crystalline sprites, a flickering cloud of anxiety and courage, positioned at key electrical substations, ready to introduce chaotic beauty into Turing's perfect logic. He felt the memory of the star-dragons, a distant, mournful song of what had been, held in his mind like a tuning fork.

And he felt the void where Spitfire should be. A cold, silent spot in the chorus.

"He's starting the activation sequence," Brenda reported, her fingers flying across the keyboard. "Energy readings from the lab are spiking for some reason. It's like a digital heart starting to beat."

"Hello Ladies and Gentleman!" Turing proclaimed. "I promised you a new technology, able to power not only this entire city, but this entire planet. And it will cost you nothing. All I have to do is press this button and the quantum device I've created will provide unlimited power." Turing pressed the button. "Free energy will improve livelihoods for all people—"

"He's a liar!" Harvey yelled out. "Where is Spitfire?"

Turing pointed his guards towards Harvey's direction, and as they made their way to him the ground began to rumble. The rumble turned into a shake and then a violent quake. The ground beneath them began to raise and lower itself violently.

A large portal appeared and as its light scattered into the space before them, the beings all took on their true form. The security guards turned into their dragonet form. And a very large figure appeared to come through the portal. It was the Aetherblade. The crowd dispersed quickly, people frantically waving their hands in the air and screaming at the sight of the dragonets and Aetherblade.

The giant mechanical hybrid dragon roared loudly and soared into the sky. A wall of flames erupted from his mouth, painting the land in destruction. His feet knocked over several buildings, and the sound of his mechanical wings ripped through the sky.

Harvey approached Turing. "Where is my dragon?"

"It wasn't supposed to happen this way. Honestly. What have I become?"

"We don't have time for your redemption story, Turing. Save it for the sequel. You didn't have to do any of this. Where's Spitfire? Now!" Harvey signaled to Kael to threaten Turing, and she assumed position, pulling out a large aquamarine colored dagger.

"He's in that van over there." Turing said.

Kael realized they were now in an impossible situation. This dragon was a heavily modified version of Eranthus, one of the most powerful dragons. They did not stand a chance against him. And if they somehow did manage to take him down, her world would suffer great loss. The very existence of the realm was fueled by the dragon's might. "We need to think about what to do from here very carefully." She pleaded.

Harvey ran to the van and opened the door. There was Spitfire, looking completely innocent and happy even though he had been essentially kidnapped. "It's good to see you best friend." Harvey knelt down and hugged his little dragon. He hugged him a little longer than usual, and their bond felt stronger as a result.

Turing had run over to his daughter and was trying to comfort her. "Can we go back to the Aetherium now? I don't feel well." Lily asked. A tear fell from Turing's eye. This was all his fault, and he didn't know how to protect her anymore.

The dragon flew back and forth, completely destroying entire neighborhoods. Families were hiding under their cars, trying to avoid being scorched from the dragon's breath. The Aetherblade seemed to be on a mission of its own, doing a kind of destruction that was unfathomable to any of them. The city seemed to be melting before their very eyes.

Harvey looked at Spitfire. "It's time my friend. I must bind you to save this world."

Time seemed to stand still, as the mind of his dragon melded with Harvey's own. It was as if they had known how to do this all along, it just needed to be the right time. They just needed to be pushed to use their true powers, and here they were.

When their minds linked, Harvey could hear a musical tone. It was deep and comforting, and thoughts of unity came to his mind. He heard an odd sound and realized his eyes had been closed. The sound was of skin stretching and tearing. He opened his eyes and saw Spitfire, and he was growing right before him. A spontaneous growth spurt! The dragon was now the size of a bus-and still growing!

Harvey stepped back to get out of the way of his growing friend. Spitfire let out a roar that shook all of them. "No way–" Harvey said, shocked that this was happening. The Aetherblade heard the roar and turned around, immediately gunning towards the sound. All of their mouths were wide open, seeing Spitfire now larger in size than the Aetherblade.

Spitfire leaped into the air and flew towards the Aetherblade. The two colossal dragons collided and the shock wave was palpable to everyone and everything. The behemoths battled and roared against each other, the sound of claws into scales ricocheted through the city streets.

Spitfire unleashed sharp claws and dug them into the Aetherblade, ripping out its heart. It fell to the ground causing a mild earthquake. Spitfire looked around and saw everything was on fire. He sat up on his hind legs, and arched his head back. He suddenly was spewing forth thousands of gallons of gelatinous goo, the dragon's spit was being used to stop the fires. The pearlescent vomit flew high into the air, raining down all around them and covering them all in a thick otherworldly colored slime.

Leo was shocked at the amount of gooey ooze he was covered in and searched his pockets. "Where's a tissue when you need one?"

Mark wiped a thick layer of slime from his face, grinning from fanboy ear to ear. "This is totally like that one movie with four guys using massive amounts of slime to overcome evil. You know the one!" Truthfully none of them knew what movie he was talking about, it must have been an older film.

The fire was extinguished. Harvey smiled, feeling thankful that things had come together this way. He looked over and saw Turing crouched down, holding his daughter and crying. "I should have just asked you for help. I'm sorry, I was desperate. I didn't know how to fix this, and I had to save Lily. But I have failed."

"What is wrong with her?" Harvey asked.

"She is sick. Very sick."

True power cannot be taken, only given.

Harvey suddenly knew what to do. It all made sense. He was chosen as the dragonbinder, because he would know what to do right now. He knelt down beside Lily as well, and touched her hand. He thought of the dragonbinder power, the ability that he was harnessing, and knew how to use now. He focused on that power, and transferred all of it over to Lily.

She was now the dragonbinder. And she would have the ability to traverse worlds freely.

"So, you are just going to give up your power like that? And we can go back to the Aetherium, where Lily can live?" Turing was having a difficult time understanding how anyone could be so selfless.

"Yes. Because it's the right thing to do. And I have what I need here." Harvey said, looking over to his friends. Most of them were still staring at the raining globs of goo, trying to make sense of it all.

Kael suddenly used her device to open a portal for herself to return to the Aetherium. She looked at Harvey, angry and disappointed. "You may have saved your world, Harvey. But at what cost? Do you even know what you just did to my world?" She walked into the portal and disappeared.

The campus's emergency broadcast system, which usually warned of snow closures, crackled to life. Instead of an administrator's drone, it blared a cacophony of that one song, from that one movie. You know the one. And of course, Leo frantically yelled in the background about the upcoming "bookshelf uprising."

Every sprinkler head had erupted, and water slowly tried to wash away the glittering, non-toxic, and incredibly sticky drake slobber. The tiny flying sprites danced and twirled in the air, with an appropriate amount of disorienting glamour.

The perfect, silent efficiency of Turing's operation broke, and twirled into a kaleidoscopic maelstrom of pixelated pastels. Guards looked up in confusion, swatting at glittery rainbows. It was a ridiculous, beautiful, and perfectly human distraction for beings that were obviously not human.

This moment felt like the memory they all knew it would become. It was the feeling of warm scales under a trusting hand. The taste of dreamberries. The simple, uncomplicated joy of a sunbeam on a sleeping flank. It was the psychic equivalent of playing a lullaby in the middle of a nuclear launch sequence.

The Aetherblade shuddered as life left its wilted body. A discordant screech tore from its vocal synthesizers. Deep within its chassis, the captive, fragmented will of the dragonbinder Turing had harvested and dissected—the source of his power—stirred. They had been silenced, converted into data.

With a shriek of pure, unadulterated fury and joy, the Aetherblade turned its head to the ground and laid there, defeated. A jet of molten-gold fire, not of destruction, but of defiant life, erupted from her jaws, severing the wires that bound her.

The Aetherblade, its core destabilized by the rebellion within, began to tear itself apart. Metal shrieked as the captive spirits within broke their digital chains. Turing stared, his reasonable face finally showing a crack of utter, incomprehensible disbelief at the horror he had created.

●　▬▬▬▬▬　●　▬▬▬▬▬　●　▬▬▬▬▬　●

It was over.

Harvey opened his eyes. He was standing on the rooftop of their apartment with his friends, having a drink and staring at the stars. The cool night air made him think of Spitfire. Spitfire would always want to cuddle with him when it was cold like this.

He stood there for a long time, and looked out at the city. He could no longer see both worlds, just one. His skyline was no longer a jumbled, overlapping mess of parallel paintings. The glowing windows of Madison were the earthly stars beneath what used to be the crystalline spires of the Aetherium. Now he just saw smoke from the nearby coal plant, billowing out its charcoal breath into the atmosphere.

His phone buzzed. A text from Leo:

So, we saved reality. Does this mean I'm finally off the hook for the security deposit? Also, can we get some more groceries now since we saved the world? My feet are swollen from all the sodium. Ramen world problems. Over and out. -'Lil L.

Harvey smiled, knowing that for once he just felt normal. He didn't have to worry about saving the world anymore, or anything really. He could just exist, just be himself. And that was enough.

● ▬▬▬▬▬▬ ● ▬▬▬▬▬▬ ● ▬▬▬▬▬▬ ●

Kael stood on a rocky ledge, looking over a vast black hole that nested in the space where her village used to reside. The farms and families that once littered the landscape were now lost to the onyx vacuum of nothingness.

Without the Nexus Prince, there would be no way to repair the damage that had been done. What was lost was lost forever, but he could at least patch up the destruction and create a space for the world to rebuild. But there was no Nexus Prince. There was no healing from this.

Kael breathed deeply, contemplating the dark rage that filled her soul. The lives of all those lost danced around in the hopeless glimmer in her eyes. She would avenge the fallen. But who would she even bring this vengeance to? Who was responsible? Surely, Harvey was just a boy. A human half-wit, at that. Not that it was any excuse, but he didn't know any better. Turing? There was always a Turing. There was always a power hungry maniac, careless to the plight of others. In every world, in every time.

She looked into that abyss, knowing that without the might of Eranthus to hold it at bay, the creatures of the darkness would emerge. Werewolves, blood drinking vampires, sirens, the undead, all kinds of evil would creep from the shadows, making the world of the Aetherium their new hunting ground. Kael rubbed her finger along the edge of her blade, knowing it was just a matter of time before she would need to use it.

15

Beneath the Dimly Lit Bridge of an Abandoned Starship

The funeral procession for Linus had begun. Harvey had expected a small and simple funeral, and now he realized his thinking was faulty. He had never seen so many people in one spot before. People of all different sizes and types, beings from all different planets and realms.

Fairies and other winged creatures sang a beautiful hymn from the stage. Beautiful multi-colored flowers adorned the entryway

Harvey looked around and saw poems and photographs, hanging to display fragments of beautiful memories in time. It was more of a memorial service than a funeral, Harvey determined. He also did not notice a casket, which he found disappointing. He really wanted to see his friend one last time.

"How did you know Sir Linus?" A stranger's voice asked, someone who was standing to the left of him.

"Oh, he was just a friend of mine." Just a friend? That wasn't entirely true. He was a very dear friend, not just a friend. "He was a good friend."

"He was a good music teacher too! He taught me how to play piano." The stranger said. They were a perfectly normal looking person, but suddenly a mouse appeared on their shoulder.

"He taught me how to play kazoooooo!" It squealed in joyous memory.

Harvey cracked a half-smile. That sounded like Linus alright.

"He was my doctor." A young woman with crutches overheard their conversation and chimed in. " I only just met him fairly recently, but he took such good care of me. Such a kind fellow."

Harvey's face curled in slight shock. He was a doctor too? Hmm, he didn't remember that being on the list. I guess it really wasn't that surprising, as Linus seemed fully capable of doing literally anything.

An elderly woman sitting nearby interrupted his thoughts. "Oh he sure was a kind fellow! He called me every day to check on me, which meant a lot since my family isn't here anymore."

"He was an avid hunter, that's for sure." The gentleman next to him chimed in.

Suddenly the ruckus began to grow into a hum of an audience as everyone began sharing their connections to Linus. And from the sounds of it, there were many connections, enough to fill several volumes of books. But perhaps that will be left for the sequel, or the threequel, if we should be so lucky as to sell that many copies. Mayhaps the Universe shall gleam the beam of luck this time, mayhaps.

"I still think this is completely unnecessary. If he's dead, why would he care?" The familiar voice of Leo. He looked at him with earnest, caring eyes. He wasn't being cold, he just handled grief differently in his culture, apparently.

"It's not about him. That's the thing. When we lose someone, we lose a part of ourselves. It's not really them we miss, for all we know he could be in a much better place."

An old woman suddenly tapped Harvey on the shoulder. "Oh, dearie." Harvey realized it was probably time for him to leave behind the Aetherium forever. Magpie Maggie must have come to escort his mind back to reality.

"Will I ever see any of this again?" Harvey had always just wanted to be normal, but now his heart was terrified at that outcome.

"I don't think you will, love. Oh, I think your world needs you now. Something ancient and evil has awakened, you see. Not like Turing, this evil cannot be reasoned with. It does not have any humanity, or aetherity either, for that matter. Oh, I'm afraid. Oh, I'm afraid for both our worlds. The darkness comes now. Ordinary men like you, oh, you will be needed now more than ever. And you can do more than any hero, king, or magician ever could. Everyday kindness, don't ya know. Yes, oh."

Harvey, Brenda and Leo looked at each other and suddenly all the magic disappeared. All the beings from the Aetherium, gone. Vanished right before their eyes.

They found themselves in an empty funeral home, where there was no funeral. And a knock tapped on the door, three times.

In walked a man in a black suit. He was tall and muscular, and looked terribly serious. "I'm Agent Hawthorne." The man said. "I would like to ask you some questions about the incursion."

The man held up a photo that was clearly the two of them, during the battle against the Aetherblade. "Oh, that's definitely not us. Looks fake to me. I have an alibi. It's a piece of furniture, but a reliable piece of furniture, I can assure you."

The man did not smile. "We will be in touch, then."

● ▬▬▬▬▬▬ ● ▬▬▬▬▬▬ ● ▬▬▬▬▬▬ ●

Hours later, after they had finished being interrogated (which lead to nothing), Harvey walked back in to his home, carrying a bag of groceries. Doing something mundane and normal again was a welcome feeling.

"Hey welcome home, Harvey." Leo said. Brenda and Mark were there too, baking cupcakes to have a surprise birthday party for Harvey.

Harvey saw Leo's niece Iliana sitting in the corner, playing with Harvey's stuffed purple plushie toy. A warm smile overcame him, thinking of the memories and adventures he had had with his friend Spitfire. He realized the time had come to pass the torch.

Leo saw what was unfolding and offered "Oh sorry, Harvey. I didn't notice she was playing with Spitfire. I can take it away."

Harvey interrupted him, "Oh, no need. Harvey went over and sat down next to Ilyana. "Do you like this silly little purple dragon?"

"Yes, he's my favorite." She replied.

"He's yours now. Make sure you take good care of him. His name is Spitfire, the Mighty. He's a purple star-dragon from the land of Aetherium."

"Wow!" Ilyana proclaimed, as she hugged the plushie dragon fiercely, her eyes glistening with joy.

●　▬▬▬▬▬▬　●　▬▬▬▬▬　●　▬▬▬▬▬　●

Beneath the dimly lit bridge of an abandoned starship, laid the **Nexus Prince**. He had no memory of who he was, or where he had come from. Just a searing, awful headache, that seemed to throb with his very heartbeat.

"Put your hands up! Reooooowr!"

That was odd, the sound the Nexus Prince heard was the sound of a large cat.

He nervously glanced over and saw a large humanoid black cat wearing a shiny silver spacesuit. The suit was covered in many different colored pins and stripes, one of which read "Agackawackapuawua:34th Battalion."

The Nexus Prince wondered if he had hit his head, if he had it must have been a pretty severe blow. Since when do cats walk and talk and look like people? Was that normal? No, it couldn't be...

"I don't know if I'm going to be much help to you. I honestly don't remember who I am. I just am here, all of a sudden." The Nexus Prince stammered, with uncertainty. The craziest part was, he was telling the truth. He truly had no recollection of his identity.

"I am fleet officer Obscure Kitty. And you are under arrest for intergalactic piracy."

The Nexus Prince put his hands in the air, unsure if there was anything else he could do.

Obscure Kitty circled behind him and cuffed his hands behind him, then began patting him down and removed his billfold from his pockets. Inside of the billfold he saw an identification card and pulled it out. "It says here your name is Linus."

About the Author

With a unique career that spans the laboratory and the stage, **John Lucy Ash** brings a lifetime of eclectic experience to his debut novella, *The Nexus Prince*. A scientist by training, and a composer and performer of both classical and rock music by passion as indie rock artist **The Talking Tears.** He studied Sociology, Anthropology and Biotechnology at UW Madison, and he resides in Madison with his partner in their home with cherished pets.

You can connect with me on:

🌐 https://johnlucyash.wixsite.com/john-lucy-ash

🔗 https://bsky.app/profile/johnlucyash.bsky.social

Subscribe to my newsletter:

✉ https://johnlucyash.kit.com/c78b29f4cf